LEAN
YOUR
LONELINESS
SLOWLY
AGAINST
MINE

LEAN YOUR LONELINESS SLOWLY AGAINST MINE

A Novel

KLARA HVEBERG

Translated from the Norwegian by Alison McCullough

HarperVia

An Imprint of HarperCollinsPublishers

HarperCollins books may be purchased for educational, business, or sales promotional use. For information, please email the Special Markets Department at SPsales@harpercollins.com.

Originally published as *Lene din ensomhet langsomt mot min* in Norway in 2019 by H. Aschehoug & Co. (W. Nygaard).

FIRST HARPERCOLLINS PAPERBACK EDITION PUBLISHED IN 2022

Designed by SBI Book Arts, LLC

Illustration courtesy of Klara Hveberg

Library of Congress Cataloging-in-Publication Data has been applied for.

ISBN 978-0-06-303833-2

22 23 24 25 26 LSC 10 9 8 7 6 5 4 3 2 1

To the musical keys and loves in my life,

and to Mamma and Pappa, who gave me wings

FRACTAL: from Latin *fractus*, "broken"; an umbrella term for structures and patterns that are the same regardless of size—they have self-similarity and are independent of scale.

—*STORE NORSKE LEKSIKON*

THERE ARE TWELVE floors in the Abel building. Two hundred fourteen steps. Rakel has counted them carefully. There are nineteen steps between each floor. Except at the ground level, where there are twenty-four steps. That's why the number of steps is not divisible by eleven.

She has always been fascinated by stairs. L-shaped, U-shaped, or S-shaped. Helical, spiral, or straight with a landing. Escalators too. When she was small she would pretend that the steps were piano keys and take stairs by playing songs with her feet. "Nøtteliten" on the way up, "Kjerringa med staven" on the way down. If the staircase was long, she would have to play several verses to make it all the way to the bottom. She played "Fløy en liten blåfugl" too. But the last long note was scary. She had to jump five full steps at the end.

The university professors are probably hiding in their offices, since the lectures won't start until next week. The mathematicians are on the seventh floor. She sneaks down the corridor, studying the nameplates as she goes. Finds the door to his office straightaway, but doesn't dare knock. Just stands there, reading the nameplate. Jakob Krogstad. She's tried to guess who he is when she walks past the first-floor cafeteria, where the mathematicians drink their morning coffee. But she hasn't met him yet, only encountered his voice through an article he wrote some years ago about the Russian mathematician Sofia Kovalevskaya. The first woman to become a professor of mathematics. She earned her doctorate in August 1874, exactly one hundred years before Rakel was born. When Sofia was a child, she read math books in secret under her covers at night, because her father didn't think girls should be studying such things. Later she became the favorite student of Karl Weierstrass, Europe's greatest mathematician. But she died young, just forty-one years old.

Stairs are a good place to think. Everyone should have a staircase for thinking. Twelve floors is perfect. Three minutes and twenty-six seconds up, two minutes and eighteen seconds down. The time it takes her to crack a moderately difficult problem. Whistle Beethoven's *Moonlight Sonata*. Or think about the town she's left behind.

RAKEL'S FIRST MEMORY is of blue days with the voice of Joan Baez coming from the record player. Sitting on a stool by the window, looking out at the mountains, she listens to Mamma sing along:

To the queen of hearts is the ace of sorrow.
He's here today, he's gone tomorrow.
Young men are plenty, but sweethearts few.
If my love leaves me, what shall I do?

The song plays over and over, in a round, as if Mamma is trapped in a circle from which she can never break free. Because every time the song nears the end, it bites its own tail and starts from the beginning again. The melody is sad and beautiful, just like Mamma. Her black hair, her golden skin. Pappa can be drawn in lead pencil, but Mamma must be drawn in colored crayons.

Time holds its breath when Mamma sings. It stops and waits. What is it waiting for? For Rakel to find something to do, so that it can come to its senses and start moving again. So it can *run and run, but never come to the door.* Just like the riddle of the nursery rhyme.

She stares at the mountains until she recognizes all their faces. They stand there in a long, long line, holding each other's hands. The mountains are her friends, and the two she likes best are Blåstolen and Trollstolen. They lean toward each other like twins, one white, the other blue.

She's friends with the letters of the alphabet too. Not just from one side, but from all possible sides. She knows which of them are themselves through and through, like *O*, and who becomes someone else when turned slightly: Big *M*, who becomes *W* when turned on its head. Capital *N*, who becomes *Z* when it lies down on its side. Those who tend to stick together, and those who are all alone. There are grown-up letters and baby letters, but the babies don't always look like the grown-ups. She's fond of the tiny *o*. It looks exactly like its mother and is so round that it rolls along all by itself. But most of all she loves the little *i*. It often spends time alone, but it never looks sad. The little *i* is a letter after her own heart. It is itself, both forward and backward, but if you turn it on its head, it protests: *!*

Her favorite number is eight. Because she was born in August. But mostly because the number eight can be written in so many different ways. Two circles, one atop the other, like a snowman. A reverse number three first, and then a normal number three. Or in the difficult way Pappa is trying to teach her, where she starts by drawing an S, before continuing upward again in a reverse S from the bottom. And it all has to be done in a single continuous movement without lifting her pencil from the paper. She likes six and nine too, because they're twins, only one of them is standing on its head. Five and two are reverse twins, whether standing on their heads or not—but only if you type them into a calculator.

The best thing about numbers is that you can put them together. When two numbers merge, they grow and become bigger than themselves. Three plus three is six. Six plus six is twelve. Twelve plus twelve is twenty-four. Twenty-four plus twenty-four is forty-eight. Forty-eight plus forty-eight is ninety-six. Ninety-six plus ninety-six is one hundred ninety-two. One hundred ninety-two plus one hundred ninety-two is three hundred eighty-four. Three hundred eighty-four plus three hundred eighty-four is seven hundred sixty-eight. Seven hundred sixty-eight plus seven hundred sixty-eight is one thousand five hundred thirty-six. They grow so fast that Rakel almost gets out of breath. And even if she stops there, it feels as if she's hurtling toward infinity at top speed.

Mamma is also heading for infinity. The song that never ends. Rakel has to look after Mamma, make sure that she doesn't get swallowed up by her song and disappear completely.

I love my father, I love my mother,
I love my sister, I love my brother.
I love my friends and my relatives too.
I forsake them all, and go with you.

One day Rakel will manage to draw a picture that makes Mamma happy. A sun in all the colors of the rainbow. Mamma dancing, with butterflies in her hair. Before Rakel was born, Mamma lived in a country where it was never cold. Where she was friends with the language, and the alphabet had more than twice as many letters. It isn't so strange that Mamma longs to go back.

"Nobody will ever love you as much as I do, Rakel," Mamma often says to her. "Who else would have sacrificed everything for you?" And there's another thing that Mamma tends to say: "If you ever have to choose between a man who loves you and a man you love, choose the one who loves you. That's the mistake people make in life."

EVEN THOUGH RAKEL is an only child, it's almost as if she has a big brother all the same. Because David stands a head taller than her. He has dark hair, just like Rakel. And he lives in the tall apartment building, just like Rakel. But she's the only one who can see him. The best thing about David is that he's always there when she wants to play with him. They are together every single day. When the other children tease her, she thinks that everything will be okay if only she can tell David about it. And when strange words bubble and spill over inside her head, tickling her until she laughs out loud, David is the one she looks forward to sharing them with. Because David understands exactly what she means and likes the same games that she does.

If she asks Mamma and Pappa about why she's an only child, Pappa says, "We didn't need to have any more children, because we got it perfect on the first try."

Mamma says, "You cried so much and were so difficult that we didn't dare have any more."

"LITTLE SQUIRREL NØTTELITEN lives in the top of a tree." Rakel curls up by the radio to listen whenever Alf Prøysen sings this song. She knows all the verses by heart. What she likes best about Nøtteliten is the way he talks to himself so much. He's a real rascal:

Nøtteliten whispers: "Mamma, are you there?"
Nøtteliten answers: "No, indeed. I'm here."

Best of all, she likes the verse where Nøtteliten makes sure that Mamma doesn't arrive at school too late:

Nøtteliten whispers: "Mamma, you should go.
Hurry up and find your way to school right now!
Don't you rush to gather nuts that you can eat before you leave.
You should sit tight on your tree stump from the school bell calls till eve."

Rakel also tends to make sure that Mamma doesn't arrive at school too late, that she gets ready for school after dinner. Because Mamma must learn to speak Norwegian.

But then comes the part she finds completely irresistible:

Nøtteliten answers: "Yes, oh yes, oh hi.
But I think I'll have to run now, so goodbye."

It's so strange that Nøtteliten answers himself in this way. But Rakel understands that this is because Nøtteliten doesn't really have a Mamma. That's why he has to pretend to be his own Mamma and talk to himself.

But when she starts in first grade at school and has to tell the class about the song she liked best when she was little, Miss says that it's the finest example she's ever heard of the importance of correct punctuation. Because it's actually Mamma who is speaking to Nøtteliten:

"Nøtteliten," whispers Mamma, "are you there?"
"Nøtteliten," whispers Mamma, "you should go."

Rakel is so disappointed that she has to tell David as soon she gets home.

"I like your Nøtteliten better—that version is really sad," David laughs.

But Rakel feels stupid. She doesn't like Nøtteliten anymore.

RAKEL SITS IN the classroom, delighted. It smells of wet chalk on the blackboard, where Miss has written out the words they're going to learn. The letters shine so prettily when they are wet. Miss walks around, handing out the Norwegian tests she has marked. Rakel is excited to hear what Miss has to say. Because she's discovered a name she can use as a pseudonym. It is also an anagram. These words taste so wonderful that she had to say them to David the moment she found them in the dictionary.

If Miss likes the anagram, Rakel might be allowed to help her clean the blackboard afterward. And she will have to make sure not to dampen the sponge with too much water. Just enough to create a lovely clear path in the sponge's wake, the way a snowplow clears the road. And when Miss sees how shiny the blackboard has become, she will say: "What would I do without you, Rakel?" And then she'll pass a hand over Rakel's hair and call her "my dear," and . . . and . . .

But Miss says that somebody has handed in their test with a false name on it. "There's nobody in this class called Eva H. Karlberg," says Miss. "Whose idea is this?"

Rakel sighs and raises her hand. David will understand, she thinks. He will notice that the letters are exactly the same as in my name.

She shows David her test as soon as she gets home from school.

"That's great," David says. "Eva H. Karlberg. A perfect anagram of Rakel Havberg. Did you come up with that all by yourself?"

Rakel nods, satisfied, but feels sad inside as she tells David that nobody in her class understood it, not even Miss.

"Maybe you just have to give them a helping hand," David says. "Give them a hint." He adds "in cooperation with Ana Gram" under her name on the test. "There," he says. "Now they will understand. And if they still don't get it, and instead think that Ana Gram is a real person, well then the more fool them."

Rakel can't help but smile. David is the bestest person she knows. "You're the bestestest person in all the world," she says.

"And you're so good at finding pseudonyms that I really ought to call you Pseudo-Rakel," David answers.

Rakel takes a sheet of paper and starts scribbling on it. "Did you know that *Pseudo-Rakel* becomes *Loudspeaker* when you permute the letters?" she says.

David laughs. "That's an incredible anagram," he says. "But you should most definitely sign your next test with another anagram of your real name. What about Helga V. Barker? Or perhaps Alva K. Herberg?"

It's actually Mamma who needs a new name. Perhaps Rakel can come up with one for her. Something nice and Norwegian, like Gjertrud. Then Mamma will no longer have to suffer her name constantly being spelled wrong. And people might stop asking about the thing that makes Mamma sad. "Everybody here thinks I'm the kind of person who would sell myself for money," Mamma often says to Pappa.

When Rakel was younger, she wondered who would want to buy themselves a foreign Mamma. But now she starts to understand. When the grown-ups get that yucky look in their eye, she knows exactly what's coming: "Ah, so your husband must be *that* kind of man?"

Rakel wonders why they would say such a thing. What kind of man do they think would bring a girl from Asia back to Norway? And do they believe that the only way the two could have met is if she worked as a prostitute? Rakel hurries to answer for Mamma: "No, he's an associate professor. And so was Mamma too, before she moved here."

PAPPA'S HANDS. RAKEL loves to watch them as they fly across the piano keys, filling the living room with Bach. Her favorite is the chorale prelude called "Ich ruf zu dir, Herr Jesu Christ."

She gets to sit on Pappa's lap while they play Bach's two-part inventions. Rakel plays the high voice with her right hand, while Pappa plays the low voice with his left. It's as if their hands are talking to each other, as if they are in agreement. Saying almost the same thing—first Rakel with her high voice, then Pappa with his deeper one.

Then they talk over each other, but are friends all the same. This is the part she likes best, because their hands move closer and around each other, like butterflies. First she runs down after Pappa to tickle him. Then she has to run up again, so that he won't be able to catch her. It's almost as if they're playing a tickling game on the piano. Afterward, it's the other way around. Pappa's voice says something first, then Rakel's answers almost the same, only with a slight twist. As if she's teasing him a little.

Finally, Pappa plays a piece she hasn't heard before. It's variations on the name Bach: *B A C H*. Imagine having a name that can be played on an instrument. At least if you're in a country that has a note called H. Pappa has told her that in England and America, H is called B. Luckily Bach was German and not English. Otherwise he could never have turned his own name into music.

Rakel wishes that she could write her name in musical notes. But to do so she ought to have been called something like Hege or Hedda or Ebba. She doesn't like any of those names. But then she realizes that she could be called Ada and play her name every time she tunes her violin. That would be lovely. And Ada is herself both forward and backward. Unlike Iris, who becomes Siri when you turn her around. If she ever has twins, she can call them Ada and Iris. Then she won't have to decide whether it's best to be oneself backward, or someone else.

She discovers several secrets in the music. Sharps and flats. How to raise or lower the pitch of a note. To let minor pass into major and vice versa. She stands in the middle of the living room with her violin and plays "Påskemorgen slukker sorgen" from memory while Pappa accompanies her on the piano.

> *Easter morning quenches sorrow,*
> *quenches sorrow for ever more.*
> *Eternally giving*
> *the light and the living . . .*

All at once they are in disagreement, she and Pappa. There's a clash where the word *light* comes in the lyrics. Pappa shows her that the pitch should be raised right there. That this increase in pitch underscores the very light that shines through—that lifts the people up. The same thing happens at the end of "Ich ruf zu dir, Herr Jesu Christ." The piece is in F minor, but the very last chord breaks into F major, like a silent promise that the call has been heard. She loves these kinds of pieces where you can *hear* the light.

But the best thing about the notes is that they are never alone, even though it might sometimes sound that way. Pappa lifts the lid off the piano so she can see this for herself. When he plays a low C, there is a little hammer that hits the C string inside the piano, so that the string begins to vibrate. But Rakel can see that the high C string an octave higher up starts to vibrate a little too. It seems it simply cannot help itself. Pappa explains that the high C vibrates twice as fast as the low one. That's why they work so well together. And the G vibrates three times as fast. These are what are known as overtones. It's so nice that the notes are linked together in this way. That you're never as alone as you might think you are, here in the world.

MOMENTS OF HAPPINESS. Arthur Grumiaux filling all of Kring-stadbukta bay with César Franck's Violin Sonata. Pappa has brought along the cassette player, and since no other families have come to the beach for a picnic on this cool autumn day, he turns up the volume. They have the place all to themselves. Mamma and Rakel sit wrapped in wool blankets, looking out across the mirrorlike water. Mamma's eyes are shining. All of Mamma is shining as she laughs and jokes with Pappa.

The sky is striped with gray and gold. As if the music makes the clouds break apart into a luminous smile that reveals how they are golden on the other side, that the gray and the gold—the grief and the joy—are two sides of the same coin. That the one cannot exist without the other because they are inextricably bound together, just as minor and major are woven together in the music. Perhaps the sky is a painting of life itself. Mostly granite, but with small flakes of gold here and there. The important thing is to gather up the tiny nuggets of gold you come across. If I can't be a violinist when I grow up, I'll be a gold collector, Rakel thinks. "Took a little nugget of gold, with a hop-hop-skip, with a hop-hop-skip," a voice sings within her. As the nursery rhyme shows, even a little bluebird can find gold.

She takes off her shoes and walks barefoot along the beach, gathering sparkling stones. The scent of seaweed. Her feet tell her about everything they come across. About the sand that is so wet and soft, about the sharp rocks she has to watch out for, about the grass that tickles between her toes. She walks happily along the water's edge, her pockets full of the treasures she has found. But when she empties her pockets, everything has turned to granite. "You have to learn that it's only the water that makes the stones shine so brightly," Pappa says. But Rakel still tries to fill her pockets with treasure, over and over again.

Mamma unrolls the tablecloth she's brought and transforms the coastal rock into a dining table. She sets it with paper plates and plastic cups, conjures up forks and spoons too. And the smell of freshly made spring rolls. Rakel decorates the table with the stones she has found. On Mamma's napkin, she puts the finest one. The one that looks like a heart. Mamma dishes up spring rolls onto the plates.

"I'll give the best ones to you two and take the burned ones myself," she says.

"Always playing the martyr," mumbles Pappa.

Rakel hopes that Mamma hasn't heard. That she won't turn sad again, not now they're having such a good time. Mamma has been in the kitchen making spring rolls all morning. For Rakel and Pappa. Luckily, Pappa accepts the biggest spring roll.

"You're the nicest mamma in all the world," says Rakel.

She wants this day never to end, for time simply to stop moving so she can stay in this place forever. Kringstadbukta, the tiny bay between Kringstad road and the marina at Cap Clara. Rakel's bay, where she and Mamma and Pappa have their own special place, where the coastal rock has formed a sofa down by the water's edge.

FERRIES CROSSING ON the fjord. Coming toward one another, each from its own side, meeting and becoming one before they slowly slide away from each other again. Pappa calls them "crossing ferries" and times how long it takes from when the ferries meet until they part ways. Had he known the length of the ferries, he could calculate the speed at which they are moving, and had he known their speed, he could calculate how long they are. Unfortunately he knows neither of these things, but he times them anyway. "Nineteen point eight seconds," he says, satisfied. Rakel calls them "kissing ferries" and hopes that they will last for a long, long time.

THE "BLUE TOWN" with the fjord and the mountains. Rakel and David's town. Molde. Moll? D? It sounds like *d-moll*—D minor.

"D minor is the saddest of all keys," says David. "Whenever the great composers have written something truly beautiful, it has always been in D minor. Like Sibelius's Violin Concerto in D Minor. Or Mozart's Requiem. And Bach's Chaconne."

"But César Franck's Violin Sonata is in A major," protests Rakel.

"That's because the joy and sorrow in that piece are so tightly interwoven that it's impossible to tell them apart," says David. "It's as if major and minor dissolve into one another in that sonata—as if it encompasses all the joy and pain in the universe at the same time."

Like being in love, thinks Rakel. One day I'll experience it for myself, and it will be just as wild and beautiful as in the sonata.

From minor you came, but major you will be.

NOT MANY PEOPLE whistle as they take the stairs of the Abel building. Rakel wonders whether Jakob Krogstad is a whistler. And which key he walks in. When she was little, she had imagined that everybody walked around with a particular tonality, some in a major key, others in a minor one. She had mostly ambled along in a minor key. Like the Violin Sonata by César Franck. Only when she decided to play the piece herself did she discover that it was actually called the Sonata in A Major for Violin and Piano, despite the fact that it was so sad. Imagine misjudging your own key like that.

She's only heard two whistlers on the stairs so far. One of them whistled so faintly that she had to hurry to keep up so she could catch the melody. "Vårsøg," somewhat out of tune. The other she heard from several floors away—a chorale prelude by Bach, "Jesus bleibet meine Freude." One of the pieces Pappa often played for her when she was small.

If she'd had a friend who was good at whistling, they could have whistled the *Moonlight Sonata* in two-part harmony. It's a difficult piece to whistle alone, because the underlying chords are just as important as the melody. But it isn't impossible. She just has to cheat a little. Whistle the broken chords while smuggling in the notes of the leading part. The extended echo of the stairwell helps her. Camouflages the notes she has to leave out.

. . .

In the square outside stands a statue of Niels Henrik Abel, the greatest mathematician Norway has ever produced. One of world history's most exceptional talents. Abelian integrals are named after him, as are Abelian functions. Like so many geniuses, he died young. Just twenty-six years old. Seven years older than Rakel is now. What will she have accomplished by the time she turns twenty-six?

The university's buildings are named after scientists. The math lectures will be held in the Sophus Lie auditorium and the group sessions in the Vilhelm Bjerknes building. She's done a trial run for walking there already. Has carefully studied the lecture list, and created a number of alternative timetables.

The mandatory philosophy lectures will be held in auditorium 2 in the chemistry department. On the tour they were given by student guides, they'd been led down into the basement of the physics department. A labyrinth of corridors wound their way to auditorium 2 in the chemistry building. Afterward, she had tried to walk this same route alone, but ended up getting lost. She only just made it out again, the same way she'd come in. She'll have to do what Hansel and Gretel did. Sprinkle breadcrumbs after herself along the corridors so that she can find her way out. And should she still get lost, she can think of something funny. Until the cleaning lady eventually finds her.

JAKOB KROGSTAD WILL be delivering the lecture series on discrete mathematics. Rakel is rather discreet by nature, and thinks she'll like this course better than the one on continuous functions in higher dimensions and multiple integrals. She has never liked integrating. Counting is much more fun.

She loves the course. To finally learn how to count all the combinations and permutations she's always enjoyed playing with. To be able to calculate the number of possibilities that exist in the world. How many different ways the letters in the word *jabberwocky* can actually be arranged—19,958,400. Or how many ways you can distribute colored balls into various containers. Different balls in different containers. Different balls in identical containers. Identical balls in different containers. Rakel wants to systematize what she has learned and creates an overview of the various problems for herself.

In doing so, she discovers that the only thing she doesn't know how to count is the number of possibilities for distributing identical balls into identical containers. No matter how she approaches the problem, she doesn't understand how it can be done. In the end she becomes so desperate that she forgets how shy she is and pounces on Jakob when she sees him sitting in the cafeteria one day, scribbling down notes on some napkins.

"Excuse me. Could you please explain to me how you distribute identical balls into identical containers?" asks Rakel.

Jakob glances up, his face taking on the same expression as that of the bus driver when she'd insisted on buying an adult ticket earlier that morning. But he gestures to indicate that she can take a seat in the chair beside him.

"Yes, I'm sure that's no problem," he says, tugging on his earlobe. "We just go like this . . ."

She watches as he scribbles away on her notepad.

"It seems it isn't so easy after all," he says, starting on a new sheet.

Rakel gets excited. "I think I tried that already, but I didn't get anywhere with it," she says.

She suddenly feels alarmed at how this might have sounded—what if he's offended? He casts a glance at her, but she only stares intently at the sheet of paper.

"Then we'll have to try something else," he says. "Do you have any suggestions?"

"I only know what I've tried, and why it doesn't work," says Rakel.

"That's a good start," Jakob says.

Rakel shows him what she's thought of, and he scribbles away on the notepad. But no matter what they try, they don't get anywhere.

"I think I'll have to take a closer look at this when I have a bit of peace and quiet," Jakob says finally. He hands her the napkin he was scribbling on when she turned up. "If you write down your name and address, I can send you an answer when I've had a little more time to think about it."

There's something scribbled on the napkin already, but Rakel can't make out what it is. It almost looks like some hats.

"What's *that*?" she asks.

"Just a puzzle I'm thinking of giving to some students," says Jakob. "A real tough nut to crack."

"Oh, I *love* puzzles," says Rakel, the words slipping out of her mouth before she can stop herself.

Jakob asks whether she'd like to hear the problem. She nods.

"A wizard has three apprentices. One day, the wizard has five hats with him—three blue and two red. He asks his apprentices to close their eyes, and then sets a hat on each of their heads. Then he hides the last two hats and asks his apprentices to open their eyes again. The apprentices are sitting behind one another in a line and can only see the hats of the apprentices sitting in front of them.

"The wizard asks the apprentice at the back of the line whether—based on what she can see—she can work out what color hat she's wearing. She can't. So the wizard asks the apprentice in the middle, but he too is unable to say what color hat he's wearing. Then the apprentice at the front of the line says, 'Now I know the color of my hat!' What color hat is she wearing?"

Rakel breathes out, relieved. "It's blue," she says.

"And you're sure about that after just three seconds?" asks Jakob, seemingly wondering whether she's just guessed.

"Yes. Since the apprentice at the back doesn't know the color of her hat, both apprentices sitting in front of her can't be wearing red hats, because then she'd know that her hat was blue. And since the apprentice in the middle doesn't know the color of his hat either, the apprentice at the front can't be wearing a red hat, because then the one in the middle would know that his was blue."

Jakob looks astonished. He asks whether she's heard the problem before. She shakes her head.

"But I enjoyed solving those kinds of problems in high school," she says. "I used to listen to *Good to Know* on the radio, and they'd offer up a different puzzle to solve every Saturday."

"Now I know who I can test out my mathematical puzzles on in the future," says Jakob. "If you manage to solve them in twenty seconds, I'll know they're reasonable weekly tasks to assign."

. . .

Rakel realizes that the cafeteria is almost empty—she's wasted a lot of his time. She hurries to write her address on the napkin, thanks him for his help, and pretends she has an appointment to get to. Jakob calls after her that he'll send her an answer as quickly as he can.

The letter arrives in her mailbox the very next day:

Blindern, March 28, 1994

Dear Rakel,
You have excellent taste in problems! Your question centers around a famous classic problem to which there is no simple solution, but I've enclosed an article for you to read. If you drop by my office one day, I'll find some more reading material for you.

Best wishes,
Jakob

PROBLEMS RARELY ARRIVE one at a time. Jakob gives her several exercises to chew on. She becomes a regular guest at his office, and because he believes so absolutely and completely that she'll solve the problems he gives her, she has to work harder, not stopping until she figures out the answers. There is no other option. He answers all her questions as though they're the most sensible questions he's heard in a long time. As if she has a special sense for asking the right questions—as if the ability to ask the right questions is actually more important than being able to answer them. *You have excellent taste in problems.* He's the first person to make her feel that her name is Rakel because she's actually a *mi-rakel*—a miracle—no matter how small.

Jakob lends her books too. And not just books about mathematics. He seems just as interested in literature as he is in math. She starts to dream that one day she'll be able to visit him at home and see which books fill his bookshelves. *Tell me what you read, and I'll tell you who you are,* she thinks.

One of his favorite poems is by Thomas Hardy, and he quotes from it for her: *I, an old woman now, raking up leaves.*

Rakel has never heard of Thomas Hardy. She tries out the lines: *I, an old woman now, raking up leaves.* The words feel curiously familiar, although she in no way feels old just yet.

"That's how I feel," says Jakob.

"With the emphasis on *old* and not on *woman*, presumably?" teases Rakel.

He laughs.

When she was small, she loved collecting leaves in the autumn, gathering them into a huge pile on the grass before they lost their color. And then running through the heap of leaves at top speed, making them whirl up into the air to form a dancing, multicolored symphony all around her. Like being at the center of a rainbow composed of red, orange, and yellow. Watching the leaves settle on the ground again, as if in a candescent painting.

She refrains from telling Jakob this. Instead, she tells him about a rhyme she read on the cubicle wall in the girls' restroom down in the basement of the Vilhelm Bjerknes building. It's so grotesque that they have to laugh:

Mary held her little daughter twenty minutes underwater,
Not to save her life from troubles, but to see the funny bubbles.

It reminds her of when the boys in her elementary class cut an earthworm into several pieces to see whether the pieces would survive. Or when they pulled the legs off a daddy longlegs to see how many legs it could live without. No. It reminds her of cutting an earthworm into so many pieces you're certain none of them will survive, or of pulling *all* the legs off a daddy longlegs.

RAKEL HAS FOUND an exercise she doesn't understand in the English math books Jakob has lent her. It seems meaningless. She doesn't understand what she's supposed to differentiate. So far, she's only differentiated functions. To study how steep the graph is, how quickly it grows, where its peaks and troughs are. She's good at double differentiating too. Finding out which way the graph curves, whether it's convex or concave. But in this exercise, it seems she has to differentiate something else. She just doesn't understand what, or how.

"The English word *derive* doesn't mean 'to differentiate,' like the Norwegian verb *å derivere*," says Jakob. "It means 'to deduce.'"

Rakel blushes. She's always had a talent for misunderstandings. They're probably one of her greatest talents.

She has a talent for slips of the tongue too. Especially when she gets excited. Then the letters and words come out helter-skelter. When she was small, she called the *Nutcracker Suite* the *Nutsacker Cruite*. Or the *Nutracker Scuite*. *Twin primes* become *prim twines*. She could have rattled off different versions of the poem "Jabberwocky" as if on a production line. But Jakob takes it all in good humor.

"I found out which graph the way curves," says Rakel. "No, I mean—which way the graph curves."

"Did you find the exercise to the other answer as well?" asks Jakob.

"Yes, I found the answer to the other exercise," laughs Rakel.

Some of the best things in life are a result of misunderstandings. When she was little, she misunderstood the children's song about the fox that hurried over the ice. She had thought that it hurried over the *rice*, and had been happy that she wasn't alone in eating rice for dinner. All the other children ate potatoes. But the fox gobbled down rice—just like her.

RAKEL STANDS IN the basement level of the student bookshop. She's just tried to stack the twelve volumes of *In Search of Lost Time* in such a way that she'll be able to carry them up the stairs to the cashier and pay for them. And she's just discovered it's impossible. She can't carry all the books at once. They're on sale, the hardback editions, at forty-nine kroner per book. It's a bargain. There's a risk the books will be sold out if she returns to buy the rest of the series later. She starts to count how many copies remain of each volume, so she can buy the volumes with the fewest left first and ensure the greatest chance they'll still have the ones she needs when she comes back.

In the midst of her calculations she gets the feeling that someone is looking at her, amused. She glances up to catch sight of Jakob standing there, watching her.

"Shall I help you carry them, so you can buy all the volumes at once?" he asks. But then he adds, "These books are absolutely wonderful." His eyes well up as he says it.

She's always thought the word *wonderful* too big to be used. She'd felt queasy when Ibsen's Nora told Helmer everything was "wonderful" in Norwegian class in high school.

JAKOB SAYS THAT he's working on a novel about Sofia Kovalevskaya. He's started to study the correspondence between Sofia and her mentor in Berlin, Karl Weierstrass. It's all in German and mainly consists of the letters from Weierstrass to Sofia, since most of the letters written by Sofia were burned. But Jakob can give Rakel a copy, if she'd like. The greatest mystery he's hoping to solve is why Sofia gave up mathematics for six years. She moved home to Russia, cut all contact with Weierstrass, and started to write fiction instead. Jakob doesn't understand how Sofia, who had always had such a passionate interest in mathematics, could have suddenly lost all enthusiasm for the subject.

Rakel thinks she'll help Jakob with this. She'll find out why Sofia stopped practicing mathematics. It's the least she can do for him, as he's already done so much for her.

"It's clear from the letters that Weierstrass was very fond of Sofia," Jakob says. "She had a special place in his heart. He admired her beauty, intellect, ingenuity, and wit—he paid special attention to her. But there's nothing to indicate that there was any romantic relationship between them; at least, if there was, it's a well-kept secret. They've left no trace of it in any of their letters. He probably saw her as an intellectual daughter."

An intellectual daughter. It sounds like the loveliest relationship Rakel can possibly imagine.

. . .

But after a time Rakel finds out that Jakob has misled her, whether consciously or unconsciously. Perhaps he simply hasn't read the letters in which it's clear that Weierstrass has romantic feelings for Sofia and is taken by surprise when he finds out she's already married. A pro forma marriage, which she entered into so she could travel abroad and study without her parents' consent.

But Weierstrass dreams of Sofia all the same. In her he has found a kindred spirit, someone with whom he can share his deepest interests and visions. At the end of one of his letters to her, dated August 20, 1873, he writes:

> Hiermit, Liebe Sonia, schliesse ich meinen Brief über mich. Hoffentlich bist Du jetzt auch der Züricher Atmosphäre entronnen, und athmest die freie Luft der Berge. Ich habe während meines hiesigen Aufenhalts, sehr oft an Dich gedacht und mir ausgemalt, wie schön es sein würde, wenn ich einmal mit Dir, meiner Herzensfreundin, ein paar Wochen in einer so herrlichen Natur verleben könnte. Wie schön würden wir hier—Du mit Deiner phantasievollen Seele und ich angeregt und erfrischt durch Deinen Enthusiasmus—träumen und schwärmen, über so viele Rätzel, die uns zu lösen bleiben, über endliche und unendliche Räume, über Stabilität des Weltsystems, und all die anderen grossen Aufgaben der Mathematik und Physik der Zukunft. Aber ich habe schon lange gelernt, mich zu bescheiden, wenn nicht jeder schöne Traum sich verwirklicht.

It takes Rakel some time to translate the text into Norwegian. It's been a while since her high-school German classes.

> Herewith, dear Sofia, I end my letter about myself. You have by now hopefully escaped the city smog of Zurich and are

breathing the fresh mountain air. During my stay here I have thought of you very often, and imagined how wonderful it would be to spend a few weeks in these beautiful natural surroundings with you, my heart's dear friend. How beautifully we could dream and fantasize, you with your fanciful disposition, and I encouraged and refreshed by your enthusiasm. So many mysteries remain for us to solve—about finite and infinite space, about stability of the world system—and all the other great future problems of physics and mathematics. But I have long since learned to temper my excitement, for not all beautiful dreams become reality.

There is a sincerity in Weierstrass's letters. Although they're mostly about mathematics, it is the few lines in which he addresses Sofia directly that contain the most beautiful poetry. He calls her "Meine Schwäche"—"My weakness." He can't help but worry about her and long for letters from her when she's not close by. He repeatedly asks her to write to him as quickly as possible. In a letter dated April 25, 1873, he writes:

My dearest, most precious Sofia, be assured that I will never forget that it is thanks to you, my student, that I have gained— not only my greatest, but my only true friend.

And it is in a letter to Sofia, dated August 27, 1883, that Weierstrass compares mathematicians with poets:

A mathematician who is not also a poet will never be a complete mathematician.

Although the letters from Sofia have not survived, it is clear that the affection was mutual. Weierstrass was the most faithful and supportive friend Sofia could ever have wished for. In her memoirs, Sofia described how important this correspondence with Weierstrass had been to her:

> *These studies had the deepest possible influence on my entire career in mathematics. They determined, ultimately and irrevocably, the direction I would follow in my scientific endeavors. All my life's work has been carefully undertaken in Weierstrass's spirit.*

RAKEL SITS AT the back of the large auditorium named for Sophus Lie. The second greatest Norwegian mathematician after Niels Henrik Abel. The auditorium has space for over six hundred students, but most still seem to find someone familiar to sit next to. If everyone took a seat randomly, there would be little probability of ending up next to someone you know. She tries to define the problem more precisely for herself: A student has spoken with three of her six hundred fellow students. Assuming that all the students sit in a random seat in the lecture hall, how many lectures must the student attend on average before she ends up sitting next to one of the three people she has spoken to?

Jakob is just completing a long proof on the board. Several of the students look as if they've fallen asleep. But Rakel loves mathematical proofs. Anything you can be sure of in the world is safe—and in mathematics you can be sure of everything that is proven. Her favorite proofs are those by contradiction, where you start by assuming the opposite of what you want to prove, and show how this leads to a self-contradiction. This means the assumption you made must be wrong, and therefore the opposite must be true. And it was, after all, actually the opposite you wished to prove.

The real number system consists of both rational and irrational numbers. Rational numbers can be written as fractions, but no irrational number can be written as a fraction. It's easy to prove that the sum of a rational and an irrational number will be irrational using a proof by contradiction. Because if the sum was rational, it could be written as a fraction. But then the irrational number you started with could be expressed as the difference between two fractions and would therefore be a fraction itself. And that is a self-contradiction. It's therefore impossible for the sum to be rational.

The irrational always wins out over the rational in this world. She knows she'll have to speak to people to make friends. But still she doesn't speak to anyone.

Math lectures can be the most boring thing in the world if the lecturer isn't able to communicate the poetry of it all and simply reads out the symbols as he writes them on the board. But Jakob has a unique ability to explain mathematics. She tries to put her finger on exactly what it is he does.

The first thing she notices is that he animates the terms. "Poor little epsilon, he's just so small," says Jakob. "But at least he rules over delta, who's even smaller." This makes it easy to remember that epsilon and delta stand for small quantities, and that epsilon is the boss, setting requirements that delta has to fulfill. Jakob is like an actor performing in a play, using both voice and body language to impart what he wants to say.

But most of all he's like a spider. It's as if he's weaving a web for them, where the points of intersection are the theory and the threads the connections he draws between the various parts of the material. The math teachers she had at school focused on stuffing as much theory as possible into the heads of their students—that is, as many points of intersection as possible. But Jakob shows her that it's not the number of intersection points that's important—the secret lies in the number of threads that bind them all together. It's these connecting lines that show her the links, that enable her to re-create the theory herself later using only a few points of intersection.

"IT'S BEEN A while since I last saw you," Jakob says.

"Well, I borrowed so many books from you last time I'm still not done with all of them," says Rakel.

She glances at her watch. Five past four. The underground train leaves in seven minutes. She presses the button to call the elevators and stares impatiently at the signs that indicate where they are. If only they wouldn't stop at so many floors today, since she has a dentist appointment to get to.

"One of them is out of order," says Jakob. "But at least it looks like the other two are on their way."

"Do you think it would be quicker to take the elevator that comes last?" asks Rakel.

"It's surely most natural to take the first one to arrive," says Jakob.

"I just thought that might not be a given, because it's less probable that the last elevator will have to stop on the way down," says Rakel.

They step into the first elevator to arrive. Jakob's eyes have a thoughtful cast.

"It's definitely not quicker on the first floor," he says, "because then the elevator doesn't have anywhere else to stop."

Rakel thinks for a moment. "That means it might be worthwhile on the second floor then," she says. "If there's more than a fifty percent chance of the first elevator having to stop on the first floor, then of course in most cases the second elevator will win."

"This is starting to get interesting," says Jakob. "What about the third floor? That isn't so easy, because then the elevators can stop on both the first and second floors."

Rakel pushes aside the hair that has fallen across her forehead. "No, that isn't so easy . . ."

"But it should be possible to work it out," Jakob says. "If, to keep things simple, we assume that the elevator that arrives at a floor first stops with probability p, and the other one then passes by . . . That should actually provide us with a fairly clear expression."

Rakel becomes excited. "Yes—because it would be better to take the second elevator if there are people waiting to take the elevator on an odd number of floors, but not if there are people waiting on an even number of floors. So that's what we have to calculate the probability for."

She thinks a little while longer. "Do you think it would be worth taking the last elevator if there's an odd number of floors between us and the exit?"

Their elevator has reached the ground floor without having stopped even once.

"In all likelihood, that would depend on how great the probability p is—but you could work it out, of course," says Jakob in a playful tone.

"That was a nice exercise," says Rakel. "I'll stop by your office when I've figured out the answer."

As usual, Jakob lets her exit the elevator first. She wishes she didn't have to run to catch her train.

RAKEL IS TAKING a course in project work for second-year students. She has to give a presentation about the golden ratio, the magical division ratio that recurs everywhere in nature—in sunflowers, pine cones, and seashells—as if it is written into the musical score of the universe itself that this is the most harmonious way of dividing a line segment into two parts: the ratio between the longest and the shortest parts shall be equal to the ratio between the entire line segment and the longest part. This is how the elbow divides the arm from the shoulder to the fingertips, how the navel divides the body from the crown of the head to the soles of the feet. Throughout history, visual artists have used the golden ratio in their artworks, because the human eye associates beauty with precisely this ratio.

She asks whether Jakob might like to hear her presentation in advance, like a sort of dress rehearsal. She trusts his gut feeling. If he thinks her presentation is good, she can be absolutely certain that it's good. And by watching his facial expressions as she speaks, she can tell that he thinks she's made the right choices, that the focus of her material and the balance of the presentation are as he thinks they should be.

"I should probably stop calling you 'the girl with the golden eyes,'" Jakob teases. "From now on, you'll be known as 'the girl with the golden ratio.'"

"There must be a sort of mathematical musicality," says Jakob, "a kind of absolute, logical ear. I've long had my suspicions about it, but after meeting you, I've become almost certain. The way you do mathematics—it's as if you immediately capture the fundamental tone of the material. While the rest of us are practicing our scales, you go straight to the music, right to the very core. I think it has to do with a sense for connections, a sense for underlying structures. The point isn't to play all the notes perfectly. The point is to know how to unite them, to find the right phrasing, what's significant, the accentuation of the various parts."

Rakel starts to feel worried. She isn't a mathematical prodigy. Jakob has far too high an opinion of her. He'll soon discover that he's mistaken, that she isn't as talented as he supposed. What if he's disappointed? If he only knew how stupid she is. How much time she spends trying to understand things.

WHEN SHE WAS small, she loved rhymes consisting of long strings of numbers that grew so fast they gave her the feeling of speeding toward infinity. The "aunties" at kindergarten would write out sums in the sand to check whether her sequences were right. Luckily they'd stop long before they got to one thousand five hundred thirty-six.

Once, she was allowed to accompany Pappa to the great mathematics conference in Helsinki. There she met the old mathematics professor. The man who was born on the same day she was, just fifty years earlier, so that when she turned four, he turned fifty-four. Pappa told him about the rhymes made up of the strings of numbers that Rakel loved so much.

But the mathematics professor didn't ask, "What's three plus three?" like everybody else tended to. Instead, he asked, "What's one and a half plus one and a half?"

Rakel was suddenly unsure. She didn't really know what "one and a half" was. Only that it was more than one and less than two. Right in the middle perhaps. But one plus one was two. And two plus two was four. So one and a half plus one and a half might be halfway between two and four. And halfway between two and four was three. If the answer was three, the next question would be "What is three plus three?" and she'd be back in the sequence of her rhyme.

She took a chance and answered, "Three."

The mathematics professor nodded, satisfied. As if he thought this was more impressive than the fact that she could rattle off the entire long sequence of her ditty by heart.

JAKOB TEACHES HER that there isn't just one kind of infinity. There is an infinity of infinities, and some infinities are more infinite than others. Mathematicians call this cardinality. The smallest kind of infinity is called aleph-null. This is the infinity you get when you take the set of all whole numbers. But it is possible to prove that there are more decimals than there are integers, so the infinity of the set of all decimals is of a greater type, called beth-one. And if you start with the set of all decimals and take the set of all subsets of this set, you get an even greater infinity known as beth-two. And you can continue to do this indefinitely.

"If I ever finish my novel about Sofia Kovalevskaya, I'll use the pen name Aleph Omega," says Jakob.

"And should you wish to pass for a female author, you can just swap Aleph for Beth," teases Rakel.

Jakob smiles. "I have the opening sentence, at least," he says. "'I sat on a bench in Bolanzo and waited for Weierstrass.'"

Rakel has to laugh. "I doubt many readers have heard of the Bolanzo-Weierstrass theorem, so I'm not sure they'll get your subtext," she says. "But it could very well become a cult book among mathematicians, so you still have the chance to reach a much wider audience than by publishing scientific articles."

HIS OFFICE WINDOW is the first thing she seeks with her eyes as she arrives at the university each morning. If the window is lit, a light kindles inside her. As if the world is a better place simply because he exists. Then the window is dark for three weeks in a row. Might he have left to attend a conference? Just as long as he isn't ill. But one morning the window is lit again. It makes her so happy that she immediately takes the elevator up to the seventh floor and knocks on the door of his office.

"I just wanted to return this," she says, holding out the book she had borrowed.

"Did you like it?" he asks.

"Yes, but I'm not sure I understood the ending. I usually like novels that have an open ending, but the author should have at least thought through some possible alternatives as to what might have happened. In this novel, it's as if the author has no idea what might have happened."

And then they lose themselves in a conversation about whether an author has a moral responsibility to have thought through at least one possible solution when leaving a novel's ending open. It feels as if Jakob has never been away at all.

She starts to fantasize about him too, as she is walking through the green fields behind the student housing blocks on her way to the university. The sky is gray-black. In an hour it will pour. She wishes that *hour* and *pour* rhymed and wonders whether she prefers the sound of "in an hour it will power" or "in a hoar it will pour," should she ever have to choose between them. She plumps for the latter alternative. It's the ring of the last word that lingers, so it's most important that the last word sounds right. Perhaps she could ask Jakob too. He's the kind of person who doesn't find such questions meaningless.

It starts to rain. If it rains as heavily as it did when she was on her way home yesterday afternoon, she'll be soaked through before she gets there. It's the kind of torrential summer downpour that can only happen here in eastern Norway. She imagines herself turning up at his office, drenched and laughing. And he'll see that she's the kind of girl who can stand to get her hair wet—the kind of girl who doesn't have to go straight home and change. Perhaps he'll be worried about her, say that they can postpone their meeting. But she'll simply shake her wet hair and say, no, it's absolutely fine—although I do apologize for standing here dripping water all over your office floor.

And then maybe he'll notice how wildly her hair curls when wet and suddenly feel compelled to brush a tangled lock from her face. And she'll see just how strong his desire is to do this—how his hand is almost moving of its own accord before he can stop it.

And she will continue to stand there in the middle of his office, trembling slightly from the cold, a little tired and disheveled, until the tenderness that fills him overwhelms him and he blurts out, "But you're soaking wet, my girl! Come here and let me feel your hands. Just as I thought—they're like ice! Let me warm them in mine."

And she will let him hold her hands and feel the warmth spread throughout her body, until she wishes she was a little girl who could crawl up into his lap, press her face into the hollow of his neck, and have the smell of his hair envelop her, so close.

But she is no longer a girl, and must simply stand there, politely, where she is.

"You can't just stand there freezing in those soaking wet clothes, you know. Come on, take them off—you can borrow my shirt for now."

And before she can protest, he's taken off his shirt and is standing there before her, stripped to the waist, and . . . and . . . and . . .

ONCE, LONG AGO, when she was in lower secondary school, Pappa took her along to a presentation about fractals—a kind of geometric object more complex than circles, triangles, and rectangles. They're similar to shapes that can be found in nature, like fern leaves, trees, and snow crystals. Fractals are made up of smaller copies of themselves, so if you enlarge a small piece of a fractal under a microscope, the piece will look similar to the entire fractal. It's as if each and every tiny part carries a copy of the whole fractal within it. Fractals are also full of holes of varying sizes, and this means that they can have a dimension that isn't an integer.

A classic example of a fractal is the Sierpinski gasket. You start with an equilateral triangle and mark the center point on each of its sides. Then you connect these center points with straight lines. This divides the original triangle into four smaller triangles—one in each corner, and one upside down in the middle. Then you remove the triangle in the middle by shading it black, so that it becomes a negative space, a black "hole." Now you're left with three smaller copies of the original triangle. You then repeat the process on each of these copies: draw straight lines between the center points on each of the sides and remove the upside-down triangle in the middle.

If you were to continue this process indefinitely, you'd finally end up with the Sierpinski gasket, which contains smaller copies of itself on many different levels and is full of holes of various sizes. This means that the Sierpinski gasket has a dimension that is not an integer. While a triangle is two-dimensional and a pyramid is three-dimensional, the dimension of the Sierpinski gasket will be the logarithm of 3 divided by the logarithm of 2—which is around 1.57.

Although she didn't understand much of the mathematics back then, she was fascinated by a figure known as the Mandelbrot set. It looked a little boring at first—like a lumpy man with a head that was far too small and a body that was far too big. The lecturer explained that the set was named after the man who had introduced the term *fractal*, Benoit B. Mandelbrot, and that spiteful tongues had said that the set actually rather looked like the man himself: Mandelbrot—the "gingerbread man."

But at the end of the presentation they were shown a film that zoomed in on details of the Mandelbrot set, as if the audience was being taken on an endless journey into it. And that was when the miracle revealed itself. It turned out that the Mandelbrot set contained an entire universe of exotic shapes, like a landscape full of seahorses and spiraling tentacles. Not only that, but ever-increasing copies of the Mandelbrot set popped up, only slightly distorted, as if shown from a new point of view.

As she walked home from the presentation that evening, she thought: Maybe this is something I can fill my life with. If I can't be a violinist, this might just be something I can do.

MAYBE BEING LOVED is like being zoomed in on. Like someone undertaking an endless journey into you, enabling you to see all the beauty you contain. That you are an entire universe of exotic shapes, with ever-increasing copies of yourself—only with a slight twist. Like fanciful variations on a known theme from viewpoints you never even knew existed. Everyone deserves to experience such a journey at least once in their life. It's the most beautiful thing she's ever known. Not only have new spaces opened up in her, but it's as if she's been drawn in an entirely new dimension. And perhaps one day she'll discover that this dimension is not an integer.

BEFORE SHE CAN make a start on her master's degree she has to get through the course in topology, which is notorious for being so abstract that over half the students fail the exam. But she is rather abstract by nature so suspects that she'll like this course better than the one on Fourier analysis and partial differential equations. As it turns out, she loves the course. To finally understand why mathematicians view a coffee cup and a doughnut as equivalent objects. To discover that something can be both open and closed at the same time.

The only thing that irritates her is that the lecturer turns up to the sessions unprepared, probably prioritizing his research over his teaching, as many professors do. He therefore stands and stares at the board for ten minutes whenever he encounters an unexpected problem. Rakel feels for him, even though it's his own fault. Had he thought through the material beforehand, he would have easily seen how each problem could be solved.

"Could you not just take a set that looks like a comb with infinitely many teeth, on which the teeth get closer and closer together, and then remove all of the farthest teeth, apart from the outermost point on the tip?" she asks finally. "This set will be topologically connected, even though it isn't path connected."

The professor nods and turns back toward the board. Several of the students turn and look at her.

"Imagine correcting the professor of topology," whispers a boy in the back row.

"ARE YOU STILL going around with the Weierstrass letters in your bag?" asks Jakob, glancing over the edge of the desk. "It must be at least three years since I gave you those photocopies."

"I've just started to look at them again," says Rakel. "And I've had an idea for your novel. You can turn it into a love story."

Jakob leans back in his office chair and puts his feet up on the desk. "I don't think one can freely make up stories about historical figures," he says.

"But it's a novel," says Rakel.

"It doesn't matter," Jakob says. "And anyway, I'd end up with the entire feminist movement breathing down my neck."

"Why?" asks Rakel.

"For a long time, rumors circulated that it was actually Weierstrass who was behind Sofia's results," replies Jakob. "A lot of people didn't want to believe that a woman could achieve such things on her own."

"But it was her work, wasn't it?" Rakel asks.

"There's no reason to believe otherwise," says Jakob. "Much of what she did fell outside Weierstrass's areas of interest."

"I'm sure they were more than just friends," says Rakel.

"If you had hard evidence, it would be quite the sensation," says Jakob. "But you have to take into account that the tone of the time was a different one—the language was much more florid. It probably wasn't unusual to write 'Liebste, theurste Freundin.'"

Rakel leafs through the sheaf of paper.

"There's a change in letter number eight," she says. "Earlier on, he uses polite phrases such as 'Verehrte Frau,' but then the tone suddenly turns intimate. He calls her 'Meine Schwäche' and the letters ooze with romantic dreams about her."

She pulls a sheet from the pile and holds it out to Jakob. He leans over the desk, wrinkling his brow.

Rakel continues to explain. "Weierstrass wrote this letter when Sofia was at home in Russia. He thanks her for the photograph she sent him, but isn't satisfied with the image. He prefers the previous photograph he has of her, and asks for a new one in another pose in which her nose doesn't look quite so big. You don't comment on someone's nose like that unless you're very close to them."

"It's not surprising that Weierstrass had eyes for Sofia," says Jakob. "But I wonder whether she was interested in a bachelor thirty-five years her senior."

"But she couldn't help but love someone who understood and supported her like that," says Rakel.

"It's a shame we'll never know what Sofia felt for Weierstrass," says Jakob. "He burned all the letters she sent him."

"That suggests they had something to hide," says Rakel.

Jakob smiles and shakes his head. "Now I think your imagination's running away with you. She was already married, remember?"

"That's true," Rakel says with a sigh.

Jakob stares into space, seemingly thoughtful. "But since the marriage was only a formality, her husband lived in another town," he says.

"But her conscience wouldn't have let her betray him," says Rakel.

"Although it's possible they had an agreement that permitted it," says Jakob.

"I doubt it," says Rakel. Then she quickly gathers up the sheets of paper, stuffs them back into her bag, and gets up to leave.

RAKEL SNEAKS INTO a presentation that isn't actually intended for students. Jakob is going to speak about the correspondence between Sofia Kovalevskaya and Weierstrass. She stands at the very back of the auditorium and hopes that nobody will notice her. Jakob's presentation is already well underway. She already knows most of what he's talking about, and is just as interested in studying how he presents the material in this kind of setting, how he once again becomes an actor rendering his audience spellbound. His charisma. The way he maintains eye contact with his spectators.

But then he catches sight of her. His eyes meet hers and turn helpless, as if to say, "You see through me; you can see how bad this is. It's just an act." And he's right in that this isn't even close to what he can do at his best. But it isn't terrible either. It's miles and miles above what others could ever do. She feels a kind of affection for him as he stands there, holding her gaze. She wants to smooth down his hair, comfort him like a small child.

She remembers the first time their eyes met like this, before he knew who she was, before she had spoken to him in the cafeteria. It was during a break between two lectures. Instead of going outside to get some fresh air as she usually did, she stayed seated, leafing through the pages of her textbook. A girl comes along, roaming randomly back and forth between the lecture hall's benches, occasionally bending down to peer beneath a bench before shaking her head and moving on. She seems to be looking for something.

"Is this the Arne Næss auditorium?" asks the girl.

"No, Sophus Lie," answers Rakel. "Arne Næss is down in the Georg Morgenstierne building."

"Have you seen the textbook I left behind this morning?" says the girl.

Rakel realizes that Jakob has entered the lecture hall and is standing there, leafing through the notes he'll go through in the next period. He glances up at the girl and says, "What's the title of the book?"

"*The Art of Critical Thinking*," answers the girl.

Rakel glances across at Jakob, who meets her gaze. He seems to be struggling to keep a straight face just as much as she is.

"No," the two of them chorus, simultaneously shaking their heads. And Rakel marvels at how Jakob's eyes reflect her, so that for a moment she sees a glimpse of herself from outside, as he sees her.

IT'S AS IF she started a new chronology when she met Jakob. As if their first meeting in the cafeteria is the new zero from which she measures time. Perhaps she should start using the designation AJ—*Anno Jakob*—instead of AD.

In the first year after encountering Jakob Krogstad, she met him in the student bookshop.

In the year AJ 2 she gave a presentation on the golden ratio.

In the year AJ 3 she took a course in topology.

In the year AJ 4 she started to study fractals in earnest, making a start on her master's degree.

What will happen in year five? *The year AJ 5.*

The best thing about this chronology is that she was born in the year 19 BJ—*Before Jakob*. And nineteen is her lucky number.

"CAN YOU TIME it for me?" Rakel asks.

"You want to do it now? Without having prepared?" replies Jakob.

"But I know how to do it," says Rakel.

Jakob shakes his head. "For most people, there's a huge difference between knowing something and being able to present it in a clear, understandable way," he says. "And the Snake Lemma is so complex that it's almost impossible not to end up getting yourself in a muddle at some point or other."

"I'd like to try anyway," says Rakel.

Jakob shakes his head again. "Okay. Fifteen minutes, then?" he says. "As a kind of record attempt?"

Rakel nods.

"Ready, set, go!" he says.

Rakel bends down and takes off her shoes.

"Well, I suppose this isn't a lemma one approaches with one's shoes on," says Jakob, surprised. Rakel pulls a chair from under a desk and turns it toward the board.

"I need all the space I can get," she says, climbing up onto the chair and starting to write, all the way up in the top left-hand corner. She starts to explain the concepts as she writes out the enormous diagram that winds across the board like a snake. When she's completed the top line she jumps down from the chair to continue.

She casts the occasional glance at Jakob, to see whether he's still following. Every now and again she takes a turn he doesn't expect. She sees that this forces him to reconsider—but that every time he agrees that's how it should be done.

After a while his gaze has changed. He seems to have stopped following the arguments—rather, it's as if he's enjoying a ballet or a piece of music. His eyes draw her to him, as they follow her hands dashing across the board, highlighting, connecting, and emphasizing the things she's talking about. Even facing the blackboard she can feel his eyes glide attentively across her body.

"Done!" she says, turning to face Jakob.

"Eleven minutes and forty-two seconds," he says.

"I did it!" She smiles.

"By a good margin," he says.

"I cheated a little bit," she says, "but the two arguments are equal."

"It was absolutely perfect," he says. "Really. Absolutely perfect."

"Not quite," she says. "I should have . . ."

He only laughs, waving away her words. "You were right. It really isn't a proof you can approach with your shoes on."

THEN COMES THE fever. It starts with the flu—it's Pappa who gives it to her. He comes to visit from Molde, the Blue City, and must have picked up the virus somewhere along his train journey. They're soon both laid up with a body temperature of 104. Pappa is well again after a week, but Rakel's fever simply won't relinquish its grasp. She tells herself that she has to be patient; she must try to keep working on her mathematics as she lies there in bed.

She can't make it to the store, runs out of toilet paper. Wonders who she might ask for help. Pappa has returned to the Blue City; Mamma will be worried if she finds out Rakel is sick. Maybe she can ask Jakob? But not until she really needs it. It's better to be afraid than to be a burden.

After six weeks, Jakob gets in touch. Asks whether she's gone away somewhere, as it's such a long time since he's seen her. Asks her to stop by his office when she gets back. He's found a mathematical article about juggling that he thinks she'll like. The juggling patterns are described using number sequences, which can be used to find new patterns to juggle. "But you have to promise me you won't get so fascinated that you decide to become a juggler instead of a mathematician," he jokes.

When he finds out that she's ill, he asks whether there's anything she needs, whether he can go buy some groceries for her. He arrives with two bags full of food—and toilet paper. She's so happy to see him that she wants to throw her arms around his neck. She hasn't seen another human being in six weeks. He says she has to go see a doctor—she must promise him she'll make an appointment for the very next day. But Rakel doesn't know how she'll make it to the doctor. She almost faints just going to the bathroom.

She tries to make it to the doctor's office, but while she's waiting for the train, she can feel it's all about to go terribly wrong. She faints. When she comes to, she can't get up. A woman gives her a soda and some chocolate; a man calls an ambulance for her. He's told that Rakel should take a taxi to the emergency clinic, but she still can't get up. So once again the man calls for an ambulance. Finally, they bring a stretcher and come and get her.

"We'll drive you home, but we just need to run a few tests first," says the ambulance driver. Rakel wonders how she'll manage to unlock the door to her apartment; she can no longer feel her fingers. The man's voice is far away. "You have a blood sugar of 1.6 and a high fever, so I think we'll take you to the hospital to get you checked out after all," he says.

At the ER they stick needles in her once an hour. The doctors can't figure out what's wrong, but it's something to do with her blood. She has dropping blood values and a declining platelet count. She can feel that she needs to pee, but gets dizzy from just lifting her head. A nurse with black hair who reminds her of Mamma brings her a bedpan. But Rakel is afraid that she's going to miss.

"Is it in the right position? Can I just start to pee?" she asks.

The nurse nods. But Rakel misses anyway, getting her clothes and the sheet wet. She can see that the nurse is angry. Rakel has created extra work for her, as if she didn't have enough to do already. The nurse tears the sheet from the bed, pulls the curtain aside, and leaves the door to the corridor open when she walks out. Rakel lies there naked on the bed, unable to protect herself from the gazes of the people walking past. She turns over. Better that they can only see her bottom.

She manages to restrain her bladder for nineteen hours, but then she has to pee again. It's a blond-haired nurse this time. "I don't know whether I can pee right—it ended up all over last time," says Rakel.

"But didn't they lift the head end of the bed so you could sit up?" asks the nurse. "No wonder it went everywhere if you were lying completely flat—you have no control like that."

And this time it's okay. Rakel wants to give the blond-haired nurse a hug.

Jakob comes to visit her. She's so happy to see him that a doctor sticks his head around the door a few minutes later, wondering what's going on. Rakel has electrodes attached to her chest to monitor her heart's rhythm, and abnormal activity is now registering on the screen. The doctor asks her to relax as much as possible, so that the values will return to normal. Perhaps medical students don't get taught what love looks like on a cardiogram.

SHE IS IN the hospital for a week. Her enlarged lymph nodes prompt the doctors to take a bone marrow sample, but they still don't understand what's wrong with her. In her discharge summary they write:

> High fever upon admission. Ketones in urine. Declining platelet count and neutropenia. Some enlarged lymph nodes detected upon palpation. Awaiting results of bone marrow sample. Collapse possibly due to insufficient fluid intake combined with viral infection.

Her condition continues to fluctuate. It's as if Rakel's body has become a sine wave, only the fluctuations are completely unpredictable. She might feel almost well for a week, only to hit rock bottom for the next three. She has to make the most of the good weeks, resting only when she absolutely has to.

She gets a first on her master's thesis. Jakob says she has to apply for PhD funding—with that kind of grade her application is bound to be granted. But she's upset when she's awarded a scholarship—she feels guilty accepting the money when she knows someone else would have been given the chance, had she said no.

She tries to hide how exhausted she is from everyone around her. She sneaks into the ladies' room in the Vilhelm Bjerknes building between lectures, because there's a sofa there. She locks the door to the lovely office she's been given so that nobody will catch her with her head on her desk, resting. She pops into the cafeteria during her lunch break, so the head of the department will see that she's at work—although she arrives late and leaves early.

She doesn't understand what's wrong with her. The doctors don't understand what's wrong with her. The sole point of light is Jakob. He brings a packed lunch and they eat in her office when she's incapable of making it down to the cafeteria. Only he sees how she's really doing, understands this isn't something she's feigning, making up.

THE KISS IN December—on St. Lucy's Day itself. She walks home through the snow like a luminous Santa Lucia. Jakob had asked for permission to kiss her. When she had nodded, he put his lips to hers. It was as if something opened, as if he was completely open to her. It wasn't unpleasant. Now she knows what it's like. It's about time. She's twenty-five years old.

"What are we going to do about this, Rakel?" he'd asked afterward. "Shall I come over to your place tomorrow, so we can talk about it?"

She had nodded.

It's snowing. Big, dancing flakes in the air. She sticks out her tongue and catches some of them. Lets them melt in her mouth, so she can experience the taste of the kissing snow.

The next day he comes over. She hopes that he'll say that he loves her even if it's impossible for there to be anything between them. It would be enough to hear that he loves her. Then she could die happy.

Instead, he takes off her top, and she feels the warmth of his belly against hers—feels that from now on she will always long to lie belly to belly with him.

"But don't you love your wife?" she asks.

"Yes," he answers.

"But then how can you do this?" she asks.

"I'm a lout," he says.

She can't believe her own ears. Really—*who is he?*

"Do you love me?" she asks finally.

"I don't know. I don't really know what it means to love," he answers. He tries to undress her lower half, but she manages to twist away. Then he gets up, and she can see there's a wet stain on his trousers.

"It's a good thing I'm going away for a few days—it wouldn't have been advisable to go home like this," he says. "And it's a *very* good thing that I put on a long sweater today."

She no longer recognizes him. He's become so repulsive. After he's gone, she thinks she doesn't ever want to see him again.

But this feeling only lasts for a few days, and then she misses him. It's so strange to return to his office. They both act as if nothing has happened. Then she feels sad, although she doesn't know why. He sees this and moves across to her. Puts his arms around her.

"Oh, Rakel," he says. "My dear girl."

FOR A WHOLE year she tries to resist his advances. From the little caresses to the way he brushes his entire body against the back of her chair as he walks past after having drunk a bottle of wine at the faculty party. It's about time he damn well pulled himself together, she thinks. But she can't help but lie close to him, belly to belly. When he tries for something more, she cries. He gets exasperated with her, says that if that's the way it's going to be, then this thing between them will have to end.

She becomes afraid, wonders what he means by that, but thinks that it's probably for the best. So she keeps her distance when they meet, instinctively backs away when he stretches out an arm to touch her. She sees the pain in his face. She can't stand to see pain in the faces of those she loves.

"I still love you, Rakel," he says.

Then she lets him hold her, kiss her, take off her top. They lie belly to belly—but no more than that. She feels interminably sad when he leaves, though she can see that he feels uplifted.

She becomes anxious. Wakes with an unease in her body. She is afraid of dying before she's experienced the act of love, but her conscience will not let her live with making love to someone who belongs to another. She will never love anyone as much as she loves Jakob. The thought of his not knowing this, and that she may never get to experience making love to him, is unbearable. But it would be even more unbearable to sleep with him if he doesn't love her. There is no solution.

She sees a psychologist for the first time in her life. "For once, try to think only of yourself, not what's best for everyone else" is the general advice she is given.

But she hasn't described what the problem is really about—she's promised Jakob never to talk about it with anyone. "It would cast me in a very bad light, were anybody to learn of this," he'd said, looking worried. She wasn't sure whether he meant that he risked losing his job.

I can't die before I've experienced what it is to make love, she thinks. But after that I could die. To make sure his family wouldn't be destroyed—I wouldn't be able to live with that. But I can do this only if he loves me.

"I can't sleep with you if you don't love me," she says.

"I love you," he says.

"But a year ago you weren't sure," she says.

"I'm sure now," he says.

WHEN RAKEL WAS little, she was allowed to help the keeper feed the elephants at the circus. But when the food was all gone, one of the baby elephants had hoped there might still be some bananas left. It eagerly stretched its trunk toward her and began to investigate her pockets. A tickling sensation ran through her entire body.

The keeper gave the baby elephant a smack across the top of its trunk, but the baby elephant was undeterred. It continued to study Rakel from head to toe with its trunk. To be examined by an elephant's trunk. It's irresistible.

Now she's lying in bed thinking that the trunk Jakob has between his legs is far too big. She doesn't understand how he'll be able to squeeze it into her.

"Like this," he whispers into her ear. "It goes in here. It can hurt a little the first time. After that, it gets better."

To open oneself completely. To be expanded from the inside. To finally let him all the way in, as deep as it's possible to go. His gaze alternates between drowning in hers and disappearing into itself completely, because he's somewhere else, in a higher dimension. It's a blind and simultaneously all-consuming gaze. Like that of a newborn baby, she thinks, and feels a great tenderness well up in her. Within her a voice sings, *You I would in rhythms fondly rivet tight.*

"Rakel. Now you're not just mi-Rakel, the miracle. Now you're *my* Rakel. *My* girl," he says. Then he falls silent.

"What are you thinking, right now?" she finally asks.

"From now on I'll walk you all the way home," he says.

Then she realizes that she cannot keep the promise she made to herself about dying. Because he makes her want to live. She wants more of this. More of him.

"I can't leave my children," he says.

"I don't want you to leave your children. I can wait for you," she says. "If you're absolutely certain that it's me you want—that it's me you can't live without."

"But the children are so small," he says.

"In eight years they'll almost be adults," she says. "Do you think you can choose me eight years from now?"

He nods.

"Are you sure?"

He nods again.

To wait eight years for him—of course she can do it. Eight, after all, is her favorite number.

IN A WAY, Rakel feels that she's cultivating the poet in Jakob. She teaches him to write poetry in limerick form. At first his limericks are fairly clumsy in both rhyme and rhythm, but they get better with practice. He sends a new limerick to her phone every single evening.

Good night, my darling, good night,
I'll hold you gently but tight.
Once you're asleep,
my promise I'll keep,
to love you slowly, my light.

Eventually he gets so good that she can give him little challenges, which he takes in his stride. "It's impossible to rhyme with *serendipity*," she says.

"Oh, is it now, Miss Fair-and-Snippety?" he retorts.

"Well, you won't be able to write a limerick with *Aphrodite* as a rhyming word," she continues.

He comes back with:

He called her his own Aphrodite
and tried to get under her nightie.
She cried out in fright

—or was it delight?—
and said that he mightn't—or might he?

Sometimes, after they have made love, he bubbles over with curious notions. "You say such strange things when you're drunk," laughs Rakel. Other times he lies there with an air of contemplation, drumming old Beatles songs on her bottom, as if her body is a finely tuned instrument. "Yesterday, all my troubles seemed so far away," or, "Hey Jude, don't make it bad, take a sad song and make it better." And in such moments he might contrive to go about proving that all lyrics can be sung to the melody of "Vårsøg."

A mathematician who loves her curves. Who says that the arc of her inner thighs makes him crazy. She's always wondered why her thighs can't behave normally and be straight, and not make this gap between them when she stands with her legs together. Now he makes her see that her thighs have the same arc as her upper arm and her waist. That they all harmonize, giving her a softness of form that seems especially attractive to those who prefer curves to straight lines—he shows her the whole. The irresistible curvature of her buttocks and the two dimples in her lower back, which she never knew existed: *fossae lumbales laterales.* And he makes her see that her nipples look like roe deer noses.

She discovers that not only is he an imaginative mathematician, but he also has a unique ability to twist and shift the entire world with his imagination, to make the most mundane observations house a fairy tale in miniature. She has the feeling of being taken inside another reality, that together they invent for themselves a reality greater than the one that exists outside.

Like when he discovers that she wears her socks inside out, so that the seams won't irritate her skin. "Well, it's good that somebody in this world understands how boring it must be for feet to be inside socks all the time. It's compassionate of you to turn your socks inside out, so your feet can feel they're on the outside every now and then too," he says.

Or when he finds out that her height is given as five foot five in her passport, but as five foot four in another document. "Yep, you were indeed born with a standard deviation," he laughs.

"wow, you really have a lot of collections of poetry by Stein Mehren," says Rakel, pulling a couple of them from Jakob's bookshelf.

"He's one of my favorite poets," Jakob says.

Rakel sits down at the kitchen table and begins to study the books' contents. "But the same poems appear in several of the books," she says.

"And the poems sometimes change from edition to edition," says Jakob.

She turns the pages. Every now and then a poem catches her attention, and she stops at it, taking her time, allowing herself to sink down into the text. Then she feels his palm against her cheek. She glances up.

"I love to watch you when you're immersed like this," he says, "when you're so lost in something that the world around you disappears."

"It must be hard to find the differences between the various versions," she says. "You have to compare the poems word for word."

"Not necessarily," says Jakob. "I only like the first version of one of my favorites. That was how I discovered that the two versions I read later were different, because I suddenly no longer liked the poem."

"You have *three* versions of the same poem?" she asks, raising her eyebrows. "Can you show me?"

"Then you'll have to take down *Through the Stillness One Night*, *The Original Landscape*, and *Collected Poems 1960–67*," he says.

She returns with the books, and Jakob flicks through the pages to find the poem's various versions.

"Which one do you like best?" she asks.

"The one I read first," says Jakob. "The one in *The Original Landscape*. But it's actually version number two. The third version is more like the original. But the third version is perhaps the one I like least."

She bends over the table and studies the text. "I know exactly what I like about the different versions," she says. "I also like the second version best, especially the questions: 'I was expected. But who?' Which version of me was expected? But I like the opening line of the first version better. And I also prefer 'A head turning like pain' to 'A head turns painfully.' Although I'm not entirely sure why."

"In the first version it's the pain that's being described, and in a way the head is the metaphor," Jakob says.

She nods enthusiastically. "Shall we each put together our favorite version and compare them afterward?" she asks.

Even though six of the lines are identical in all three versions, it is possible to create 2,592 variants by swapping out the lines that are different. After a few minutes, she's done.

"Now I'll read you mine, and then you can read me yours," she says.

Summer Passed Quickly This Year

Happiness is a recognition. But of what?
I have opened a secret door
And luminous dust falls in dark chasms.
This streaming hair. You!
A head turning like pain.
I was expected. But who?
In the dusk we set our longings
aside. To be recognized anew

Rocking them to sleep like our children
and smiling.

Summer passed quickly this year.
We leave tomorrow
For the last time walking out to the sea.
We stand on the outermost cliffs
and feel the earth growing colder and colder.

"That's astonishingly similar to my version," Jakob says.

"How so?" she asks.

"There are only two lines that are different," replies Jakob. "I prefer the opening line of version number two: 'Recognition, but of what?' I feel the version you've chosen is more closed, that it sort of insists on the happiness."

"That's precisely what I like about it," she says. "Even though the poem is about a breakup, it insists that happiness is also present. That even though there's mostly granite, the gold shines more brightly. That's also why I like the line 'This streaming hair. You!,' which isn't in any of the other versions."

"You have a point there," Jakob says. "But in any event, I prefer the line 'Rocking them to sleep like children.' I think 'our children' is far too concrete. I see the children as an image of yearning."

"That's a nice interpretation," she says. "And then it's actually for the best that there are no shared children. They have conflicting long-ings, which they manage to rock to sleep as they make love in the dusk. But it doesn't last very long. Because summer passed quickly this year."

"As has the time—it's one o'clock in the morning," says Jakob. "I suppose you'll have to spend the night here."

TO BE PHOTOGRAPHED onto someone's retinas. It's as if Jakob is taking her picture with his gaze, as if he has an entire roll of film full of images of her on his retinas. Sometimes she can feel it when he photographs her like this. She knows that he has an image of her from behind, where she stands naked in the center of the living room, looking out across the city from the new apartment she's just bought, but has not yet furnished. They have just made love, and now he must go. He has titled this photograph "Is There Anyone Who Can Help This Woman?"

He also has a picture of her walking before him into the living room on the day he visited her, bringing her food because she had been ill for six weeks and unable to buy groceries herself. The spring before he first kissed her. Her white robe falls so softly around her body, accentuating her curves. Embarrassed, he had attempted to suppress a gasp; he had to walk hunched over into the living room after her.

And he has told her that he has an image of her lying there asleep in his bed, naked under the thin sheet. She hadn't planned to stay over, and had no nightclothes with her. The day she was permitted to accompany him home to Nesoddtangen to peruse his bookcases, while the rest of his family was on vacation.

They had become so engrossed in talking about Stein Mehren that the last boat had already left. It was too late to send her home. He comes out of the bathroom and stands in the doorway, watching her. She's lying on her side. The morning light falls across the sheet that envelops her body. He stands there and looks at her curves, the sweeping arc of the iliac crest. He doesn't yet know he will fall so deeply that he will make love to her here, in his own home, in his own marital bed.

"DO YOU THINK your novel could be adapted into a film script?" asks Rakel. "So I could play the role of Sofia, and you Weierstrass?"

"First we need a novel to adapt," says Jakob. "I haven't even written the first chapter."

"But you have that brilliant opening," says Rakel. "'I sat on a bench in Bolzano and waited for Weierstrass.'"

"Oh, I'd forgotten that sentence," Jakob says.

"You have to note down your ideas as you go along," says Rakel. "But anyway, that means we at least have the opening scene. Sofia sitting on a bench and waiting for Weierstrass. In Bolzano."

"Why is she waiting for him in Italy when Weierstrass lives in Berlin?" Jakob asks.

"We can let the viewers wonder about that," replies Rakel. "Perhaps they're on a secret romantic getaway?"

"I have no intention of writing a love story," Jakob says.

"I think it will strengthen your narrative," says Rakel. "But we can figure that out later. Anyway, we cut right from the opening scene into a flashback."

"To Sofia's childhood?" Jakob asks.

"To her first encounter with Weierstrass," says Rakel. "Do you know how they met?"

"She called on him at his home in Potsdamer Strasse," Jakob says.

"Then the camera can cut straight from the bench in Bolzano to the nameplate on his door in Berlin," says Rakel. "We see a woman's hand knock on the door. The camera zooms out, and we see the building and the female character to whom the hand belongs. She's wearing an outfit from the 1800s. A horse-drawn carriage pulls away in the street outside.

"The camera zooms in again, this time on the woman's face. It's partly in shadow, but we can tell that she's nervous. The door is opened by a housekeeper. Sofia introduces herself and asks to speak with Weierstrass. The housekeeper says that the great mathematician must not be disturbed while he's at his work. The camera lingers on Sofia's face, and we understand why the housekeeper changes her mind and says that she'll check whether Weierstrass is available after all.

"When she comes back, she gives a friendly nod and lets Sofia in. The camera follows Sophia's shoes across the dim corridor. The shoes stop outside the door to Weierstrass's study."

"Goodness—you're well on your way to taking over my entire project," says Jakob.

"I'm sorry, I don't mean to take over—I just want to help you," says Rakel. "What do you think Weierstrass thought the first time he met Sofia?"

"He probably thought she was irresistibly cute," says Jakob. "And then he was probably irritated at the fact that she was wearing such shapeless clothing that he couldn't get a proper look at her ass."

"Be serious," laughs Rakel.

"You drove me crazy with those long sweaters you always went around wearing, at any rate," says Jakob.

"But seriously, do you know what their first meeting was like in reality?" asks Rakel.

"He tried to get rid of her by giving her some advanced problems that he was sure she wouldn't be able to solve," says Jakob. "So when she came back a week later having solved them, he thought she must have cheated. He asked her to explain her solution. The method she'd used was so original that he was convinced she must be the most gifted student he'd ever come across. So he offered her private tutoring at home, since the university refused to permit her to attend lectures there."

"Do you think she climbed up onto a chair and drew on a black-board with chalk as she explained her solution to him?" asks Rakel.

Jakob smiles. "It's certainly possible," he says. "At least, Weierstrass writes that she took off the bonnet that hid her face. Locks of her hair fell down, and he was struck by how young and beautiful she was. When she noticed his eyes on her, she blushed. And as she explained her solution, her eyes took on the eager, intelligent look that left such a deep impression on people."

"What kind of people?" asks Rakel.

"People like Fridtjof Nansen and Alfred Nobel," says Jakob. "It is rumored that it's actually Sofia's fault that there's no Nobel Prize in mathematics. Alfred Nobel is said to have been among the suitors she rejected."

"Why haven't you written about this in your novel?" asks Rakel.

"I'm still gathering material," Jakob says. "And I still haven't found out why Sofia stopped practicing mathematics for six years."

"They say that the art of writing a novel is to sit down and do it," says Rakel.

THE ART OF coping with the illness is not to plan too much. Then she is spared having to be disappointed. Everything moves more slowly than before—it feels as if her brain is full of syrup. She can't concentrate on her mathematics. Doesn't manage to follow the lectures. She lies against Jakob's arm as he whispers the course material in her ear. This is the only way her mind can absorb it.

The worst thing about the illness is its unpredictability. Her legs suddenly giving way beneath her in the supermarket, so she has to fold herself over the shopping cart. The dizziness in the library that forces her to steady herself against the shelves. The constant feeling of being about to faint—in the elevator, on the train, in the line for tickets at the concert hall. Jakob is good at acting as if it's the most natural thing in the world that she should need to lie down, often in the strangest places.

"Are you sure you're up to this?" asks Jakob.

"No," says Rakel. "But let's try anyway."

"There's no shame in turning back," says Jakob.

"But we've already bought tickets," says Rakel.

She's been looking forward to the performance for a long time. *The Enigma Variations*, at Oslo Nye Teater. It isn't far to walk from Nationaltheatret station. But when they cross the square at Universitetsplassen, she feels her body betraying her. She throws up down the front of her coat and is so dizzy that she has to lie down on the steps outside the University Aula.

"Just pretend you don't know me," she says.

Jakob sits down beside her, rests her head in his lap. Acts as if it's completely natural to lie here and rest in formal clothes.

"Relax—people will just think you're drunk," he jokes.

Afterward, he walks her all the way home. Wipes away her tears with his thumb and embraces her, until her body stops shaking.

"Do you think Weierstrass kissed Sofia here?" he asks, planting a kiss on her forehead.

"It isn't unthinkable," says Rakel.

"And here?" says Jakob, kissing the lobe of her ear.

"More doubtful," says Rakel.

"Here, then?" Jakob asks, kissing her eyelids.

"Only if he loved her," says Rakel.

"Where would Sofia most like to be kissed when she was sad?" asks Jakob.

"On her neck," says Rakel.

Jakob kisses her neck until her body glows. "Better?" he asks.

She nods. It's impossible to have an entirely dark view of existence while one's neck is being kissed.

SHE DREADS WEEKENDS and holidays, all the days off work when she doesn't get to see him. She doesn't have the strength to do anything but lie in bed and long for him. She envies his wife, who gets to be with him every day. Gets to hear his breath at night, feel the warmth of his back. Wake beside him in the morning. All while Rakel burrows her nose into the pillow, seeking the smell of him. Hugs the covers to deaden her yearning for him, and asks the full moon to watch over him. She wishes he could look a little sadder when he leaves her.

"Will you miss me?" she asks.

"Of course I'll miss you," he replies.

"But you don't look sad," she says.

"We've just had such a nice time together," he says. "And I'm already looking forward to when we'll see each other again."

Sometimes she wonders whether he really means it when he says he's going to choose her. When he forgets himself and talks about things he's going to do with his family in the future—like taking the entire round trip on the Hurtigruten ferry to celebrate his sixtieth birthday. She turns away.

"What is it?" he asks.

"Nothing," she answers.

"No—you're upset about something," he says.

She can't stop the tears that roll down her cheeks; buries her face into the hollow of his throat. "When you're sixty, the two of us will be together," she whispers.

"I'm sorry—I just misspoke in the moment," he says. "It doesn't mean anything, you mustn't read too much into it, Rakel."

But then he forgets himself again.

She reads the relationships column in the weekend supplement and sends a desperate message to his phone: "You're never going to choose me. The psychologist in *A-magasinet* says that married men almost never leave their wives for their lovers."

"It'll be different with us," he answers.

"How can I know that?" she asks.

"I can't let you bear the suffering alone forever," he answers. "You know that I'll choose you as soon as I can. I love you!"

"Do you ever tell her that you love her?" she asks.

"Only if she asks me directly," he sighs.

"But *do* you love her?" she continues.

"Not the way I love you," he answers. "You're the great love of my life. It's you I look forward to speaking to, to seeing every day. At home they think I'm just this silent oddball. But when I'm with you, I come alive. You know how chatty and silly I can be. I'm only that way with you."

And she's seen it herself, the way he lights up every time he catches sight of her. How he sits and waits for her with a happy, hopeful expression when they've agreed to meet somewhere and she sees him before he sees her.

"But how can I know that you won't do to me what you've done to her?" she asks.

"I'm not exactly the Casanova type," he says. "I'd never been unfaithful before I met you."

"Maybe that's because you never had the chance," she says. "That time I asked you whether you had any regrets, you said you wished you'd slept around a bit more."

"There are never any guarantees in life," he answers. "But in a way, I feel that I have to be honest with you. You see right through me. I feel that we're on the same level."

SOMETIMES IT FEELS as if her guilty conscience and shame are ripping her apart inside. Jakob finds this medieval.

"How many girls do you think are feeling ashamed the way you are, here in this country and in this day and age?" he asks. "Your mother might still be living in Asia in the 1950s, but you're not."

Rakel feels ashamed all the same. Thinks how hurt Mamma and Pappa would be if they found out she was behaving like this, that she's done something she *knew* was wrong. Maybe they won't be able to love her as much as before.

"You have nothing to feel ashamed about," says Jakob. "If anyone should feel ashamed, it's me. This is my responsibility. You're nothing but loveliness. You're the loveliest person I've ever met."

"But how can you do this to her and not feel ashamed?" she asks.

"I'm a lout," he says, smiling. "And anyway, I feel that I'm being faithful to something else. To us. That for what might be the first time in my life, I'm being true to myself. The times we encounter true love in this life are so few. I see it as a gift, not a sin. And I hope you will too, one day."

The times we encounter true love in this life are so few. And implicit in this: it's worth waiting eight years for it. Although it clearly isn't worth getting a divorce or risking the kids being traumatized.

Sometimes she wishes that time could go backward. That she could spool her life back, rewinding to the time before she met Jakob, so she'd be spared having a boyfriend who has to be kept a secret. A boyfriend who often feels like an imaginary friend.

When she was little, she had asked David whether he thought time could move backward or stand on its head.

"It can move quickly or slowly, at any rate," David said.

"What does *eve* mean?" asked Rakel.

"*Eve* is the same as *evening*," David answered.

"And morning comes before evening, right?" Rakel said.

David nodded.

"But Christmas Eve comes before Christmas morning, and Easter Eve comes before Easter morning, so I suppose time moves backward at least twice a year," said Rakel.

It's actually unfair that time has only one dimension, while space has three. Why shouldn't time be able to romp and frolic just as freely as space? If time had several dimensions, it would be able to move forward and backward simultaneously—a circular motion in which time constantly returns to the start. Then it might be possible to give yourself some good advice in critical moments the next time you passed by. But on the other hand, the world would become a lonelier place. It would be more difficult to meet each other at a given time, because several coordinates would all have to match up. It's probably best that time continues to be one-dimensional, like a straight number line.

Jakob says that the average love affair lasts for seven years. Rakel becomes afraid that this is what he's waiting for—for the love to pass, so there'll be no need for him to choose her after all. For him, it's possible to separate the physical from the emotional. But she can't be connected to someone at just a single point. She needs to be connected to the other person all the way.

"YOU'RE SO BLOODY proper," says Jakob. "You should let loose a bit more. I bet you've never so much as snatched an apple, have you?"

Rakel shakes her head. "I feel that I always have to do my best," she says.

"Why?" asks Jakob.

Yes—why? she thinks. In order to be a good person? In order to be lovable? She's been this way for as long as she can remember. Right?

"When we know that you've done your best, we can never be angry at you," says Pappa.

Rakel is a big girl now—today is her fourth birthday. Pappa has lifted her up onto the top of the wardrobe so that she's just as tall as he is and can look him straight in the eye. She feels big and proud. Pappa is very wise. Of course she'll always do her best. Then they can never be mad at her.

She keeps her promise. Every day, she asks herself whether she's done her best. Or whether she could have done even better. Knowing whether she's really done her best is harder than she imagined. Nobody can demand that you do more than your best. But your best you must always do.

One time, it all went wrong regardless. Her shoes and the legs of her pants were wet when Pappa came to collect her from kindergarten. They'd been to Kringstadbukta bay for the day, and Rakel wanted to wade out into the water to gather stones. She had just managed to take off a shoe when the kindergarten auntie said that she shouldn't take off her shoes to paddle in the water.

Shouldn't I? thought Rakel. She found this strange. She always had to take off her shoes when she was with Mamma and Pappa.

But she did as the auntie had said. Afterward, the auntie was angry at her, and Rakel was so afraid. So she said that Erik had pushed her out into the water.

"Is that true, Erik?" asked the auntie.

Erik nodded. And then he had come over and apologized to her. So perhaps that was how it had happened after all.

But when she told Pappa that the auntie said she could go into the water with her shoes on, Pappa didn't believe her. "I don't think you're telling me the truth," Pappa said. "Now tell me, what really happened?"

Rakel felt unsure. And Pappa asked her over and over again. In the end, she said that Erik pushed her out into the water. She felt a lump form in her stomach as she said this. Because Erik only pushed her *after* she had walked into the water herself. But her shoes didn't get wet until Erik pushed her *farther* out. So it was sort of true. But she still had a lump in her stomach.

Only much later did she understand. When she realized what the auntie had meant. "Rakel, you shouldn't take off your shoes to go paddling in the water" didn't mean that she shouldn't take off her shoes. It meant that she shouldn't walk into the water.

SHE HAS NEVER been good at dressing up. But it will hardly do to wear jeans and a T-shirt to the Abel Prize award ceremony in the University Aula. Jakob studies her outfit. "Do you always buy shoes in the men's department?" he asks.

Rakel nods. "They're the best shoes for walking in," she says.

"But you don't have particularly big feet," says Jakob. "Surely even the smallest men's size must be too big for you?"

"When I was little, Pappa always bought me shoes that were two sizes too big, so I could grow into them," says Rakel. "My toes are used to having plenty of space to wiggle around."

"But you must have gotten yourself some formal shoes for special occasions at some point?" says Jakob.

"I so rarely put on a dress or get dressed up," says Rakel, befuddled and peering down at the heavy men's shoes beneath the hem of her dress. "Do you think it would be better if I put on my running shoes?"

Jakob resignedly shakes his head. "Well, we don't have time to pop into a shoe store now, so you'll have to go as you are," he says. Then he gives her a cheery look. "Anyway, to those of us who have a thing for Pippi Longstocking, you're actually irresistibly cute."

According to Jakob, a frugal upbringing is the root of all ruin. "I've never seen anyone enjoy ice cream as passionately as you do," he says. "That's what happens when you bring your kids up on carrots."

Rakel licks ice cream from around her mouth. Perhaps he's right. Italian ice cream is one of her very favorite things. It's almost irresistible. She could eat three scoops of it every single day. Dark chocolate. Cherry. And pistachio or salted caramel. When she was young, she agreed with Pappa's assertion that it was stupid to eat sweets. She didn't envy her classmates, who were given candy or chocolate as a Saturday treat. An apple was much better.

But she wanted a bag of Seigmenn jelly babies for Christmas. Mamma fought for Rakel's wish to be granted, putting up with the looks she was given by the people in the store who walked past as Pappa lectured her. People who probably thought that foreign women were always nagging about sweets and needed to be told off, like children. Rakel felt so bad for Mamma that she stopped asking for candy for Christmas.

Instead, she became an expert at sniffing out where such goodies are served. During the announcement of the Abel Prize at the Norwegian Academy of Science and Letters, fine confectionery is always on offer.

There are two types of confectionery lovers. First, there are those who take their time studying the descriptions on the box in order to figure out which chocolate they want, and who then spend just as long looking for that particular chocolate, perhaps only to realize that someone else has already taken it. If so, they repeat the procedure while swallowing their disappointment at having to settle for a different kind. If the chocolate they want *is* still available, they then risk having such high expectations as to how it will taste that they end up disappointed regardless.

The other type of confectionery lovers are those who take a random chocolate from the box without even looking at it, pop it happily into their mouth, and seem to enjoy a completely carefree existence.

Sometimes people in the first category can infect people in the second with their behavior, thereby complicating their lives unnecessarily. Jakob can no longer eat confectionery as effortlessly as he used to. It's Rakel's fault. Once you've started to consider your options, it becomes difficult to stop.

"HAVE YOUR SHOELACES come undone again?" Jakob asks.

"I think I must have particularly slippery ones," replies Rakel. She bends down to tie her laces for the third time.

"But it's strange that you have equally slippery shoelaces on all your shoes," says Jakob. "Let me see how you're tying them."

Rakel shows him how she starts by creating a simple knot at the bottom. Then she makes a loop with the left lace and passes the right one around it from behind to feed it through the hole from the front, creating a loop on this lace too.

"Who taught you that?" Jakob asks.

Rakel thinks for a moment. "Nobody," she answers. "I learned it all by myself. I just copied what Pappa did."

"You do the exact opposite of what I do," says Jakob.

He bends down to show her with his own laces. The first part of the knot is exactly like hers. But then he creates a loop with the right lace instead. He passes the left lace around from the front and feeds it through the hole from behind to make a loop with that lace too.

"Our bows look very similar," Jakob declares. "It shouldn't matter which loop you make first."

"It must be the interaction with the first part that makes the difference," says Rakel, "because we tie the first part in exactly the same way." She thinks for a moment. "Perhaps the knot I make isn't a knot, but an unknot," she says. "Do you have a piece of paper, so I can investigate?"

During her first semester as a student she had attended a pop-science lecture about knots and unknots. The lecturer had shown them how they could use the Alexander-Conway polynomial to identify unknots. This polynomial will always be trivially equal to 1 for an unknot. But no knot with fewer than eleven crossing points has a trivial Alexander-Conway polynomial. Even though she doesn't remember all the details, Rakel is sure she'll be able to recall the main ideas if Jakob has a sheet of paper.

Jakob shakes his head. "Typical you," he laughs. "To be so good at abstract topological knot theory, and yet so astonishingly bad at tying your shoelaces."

THERE ARE DAYS she doesn't get to see him, even if it's neither a weekend nor a holiday. She pretends that he's there all the same. Asks him what he fancies for dinner. Would he like rice or pasta with the meat sauce? Should they go to the store before or after they've watched the evening news? The kind of everyday things that others likely take for granted.

His wife gets over a hundred hours with him every week, while Rakel is lucky if she gets five. Over the course of a year, she'll spend no more time with him than his wife does in a week. And over eight years, she will have had the same amount of time with Jakob as his wife gets in two months. But after eight years have passed, everything will be different. They'll be together forever. And anyway, time can be weighted. An hour with Jakob is worth at least twenty hours without him.

She's always been a saver. She's an expert at pushing the slice of ham atop her bread ahead of her as she eats, so she can gobble it down on its own at the end. She prefers having dreams of the future to using up her dreams here and now. On one of the rare occasions she was invited to a children's birthday party and given candy, she saved it for years. Until a white coating appeared on the sweets, and Mamma said that they had to be thrown away. This made Rakel so upset that she cried.

Now she's started saving up her time with Jakob. On the days they haven't agreed to meet, she sits in the vestibule of the Vilhelm Bjerknes building. From here, she can see his office window. When the window is illuminated, a longing is awakened within her. But she doesn't call in on him. If she lets him work now, this is time she will have in the bank. Perhaps they can go to the beach on Friday?

She waits until he turns out the lights to go home—this tends to happen between four and five. Then she hurries across to the Abel building and stares at the signs that show the positions of the elevators. If none of them stop on the seventh floor, she knows that he's taken the stairs. The important thing then is to just happen to be on them, so that he has to pass her on his way down. She spends a disproportionate amount of time on staircases in the hope that she might catch a glimpse of him. But she can't do this too often. Only when she's desperate. It will start to seem conspicuous otherwise.

Generally, she's satisfied just to see him through the window from the Vilhelm Bjerknes building as he crosses the square on his way to catch the train. She checks his teaching schedule too. So she can bump into him by chance when he's on his way to Sophus Lie to give a lecture.

One day, she regrets not being on the stairs as he leaves. She hurries after him, catching up with him on the hill that leads down to the station. Downhill, she can walk almost as quickly as she did before she fell ill. It's moving uphill that's the problem.

She's just about to pass him with a little nod when she hears his voice: "I've always admired your stride—it's rare to see a girl who can walk that fast."

She slows down. "It's because I had to keep up with Pappa when I was little," she says. "And he had such long legs."

"Why did you have to keep up with him? Couldn't he have adapted to you instead?" Jakob asks.

"I actually see it as a positive thing," she answers. "Because it meant I developed a good technique and can walk really fast now."

"Well, you do always see the positive side of things," Jakob says.

. . .

In her mind's eye, Rakel glimpses a little girl taking a walk with her parents. Pappa first, the little girl close at his heels. Mamma farther back, bringing up the rear. But then the little girl stops and waits to make sure that Mamma doesn't end up too far behind. Pappa simply hurries on. So she ends up walking alone, roughly halfway between Pappa and Mamma. There's a stretch of fifty yards or so between them.

"HAVEN'T YOU BROUGHT your swimming shorts?" asks Rakel. She can't believe that Jakob has been dumb enough not to bring his bathing suit when they've agreed to come to the beach.

"I didn't think it was a good idea to go swimming in this weather," Jakob says.

"But we always go swimming when we come to Gressholmen," says Rakel.

"We've only ever been here in good weather," Jakob says.

"But the air is warm," she says. "And I love to swim in the rain."

"It was stupid of me," says Jakob, struggling to fish out the hot-dog buns as he holds the umbrella above them.

"You can swim without your swimming shorts, then," she says after they've eaten.

Jakob shakes his head. "Not on your life."

"But there's nobody else here," she says.

"Somebody might come along."

"In this rain?"

She pulls off her T-shirt and stands before him in her jeans and bikini top. "Life's too short not to try skinny dipping."

"But what about you?" he asks.

"Well, I brought my swimsuit," she replies. She takes off her jeans and wades out into the water. "It's warmer than I thought," she cries. "Come on!"

He shakes his head.

"Just keep your clothes on until you're right at the water's edge, and then—plop! You can be straight underwater!"

He looks around and realizes she's right. There's nobody else here to see them. There aren't many people who would go for a swim on such a rainy, late August day. And if anyone else should happen to have come out for a swim, it's unlikely they would wander all the way down to this remote little bay that they've found.

She can see that he's hesitating. Then he takes off his shoes, socks, T-shirt, and trousers and clambers down from the rocks. The beach is covered with tiny pebbles, and he totters cautiously to the edge of the water. He sticks his toes into it, as if looking for a final excuse, but the water isn't too cold. So he grabs hold of his waistband and pulls down his underpants.

"Yes—that's it!" she cries.

The beach is stony and the water shallow, so he isn't straight underwater with a plop as she promised. But at long last he can cast his body forward and disappear beneath the surface.

She swims a few strokes. It's so quiet. Nothing but a siren in the distance and the sound of raindrops hitting the water.

"You're right that life is too short not to try skinny dipping," he shouts.

"Is it different without clothes?" she asks.

"Yes," he says.

"In what way?"

"Try it and see for yourself."

She rummages around under the water and then triumphantly waves her bikini bottom at him. She soon has her top off too, and glides toward him like an undulating seal pup.

"So is it different?" he asks.

"Yes," she says.

"In what way?"

"Closer," she says.

"To what?" he asks.

"Nature," she says.

Then she grasps his head tightly and kisses him. Slowly.

"I didn't know it could get hard underwater," she says.

"Neither did I," he says.

"The water isn't exactly warm," she says.

"You should take it as a compliment then."

"I intend to," she smiles, and straddles him.

It's easier than she expected for him to slip into her. The friction of the water is hardly noticeable. Once he's in her, his breath quickens; her hips grind against his. He can't control himself and empties himself deep inside her, even though he's not wearing a condom.

"I like it better like that," she says.

"In what way?" he asks.

"Closer."

"To nature?"

"No, you nitwit! When I can feel you come inside me."

"You mustn't act like an irresponsible teenager," he says.

"Why not?" she says.

"Don't ask stupid questions," he says.

She starts fiddling with her bikini under the water.

"But there's nobody here," he says.

"We're not nudists either," she says.

"YOU COULD HAVE pretty much anyone you want, Rakel," says Jakob. "I think all the boys in the department are interested in you."

"But you're the only one who truly knows me," she says. "It's you I want. Don't you understand that it isn't a cohabiting partner I need? I need so much more than that. I need a *co-poet*."

He sighs. "Have you never felt anything like this for anyone else?" he asks.

"No," she answers.

"Is there nobody else you could imagine having these kinds of feelings for either?" he asks.

She thinks for a long time. "Only the Author," she answers.

The Author came into her life that first year she became a student. She was standing in the middle of her room. The radio was on. Then something seemed to hit her in the diaphragm. It was a reading. She didn't catch the name of the book or who the author was. She just stood there, listening to the music in his language and the beautiful images he created within her. She noticed how the text expanded her, showed her spaces she never knew existed. To be expanded from the inside. It's irresistible.

She discovers him again through Jakob, some years later, when Jakob lends her a book by his favorite Norwegian author. A little way into the book, she finds the chapter she heard on the radio. And she's just as gripped by it this time too, thinks that if she could write such a chapter, then her life will have been worth living. It's as if the sentences attach themselves to her insides and continue to sing in her forever—they become part of who she is.

Later, Jakob lends her several more books by the Author, including his great romance novel, which Jakob likes above all the others but almost nobody reads. The Author has said in an interview that he regards this novel as his best, and that the day he meets someone who has read it, he will kiss their shoes. Rakel looks forward to the day she can introduce Jakob to the Author. So the one can kiss the shoes of the other. So she can show them both how alike they are—this connection in the universe, which so far only she has seen.

The first time she meets the Author in reality is at a concert at the Vigeland Museum, with the young, talented boy on violin. The one with the dark curls, who is only sixteen years old but already on his way to becoming a man who is entirely to Rakel's taste. César Franck's Violin Sonata is on the program.

A couple of rows behind her, a middle-aged man is sitting with a red-haired woman. Rakel's back is aching, so she wants to wait as long as possible before sitting down. But since it looks strange just to stand there, she peers in the direction of the entrance, as if she's waiting for someone. She feels silly, putting on this performance for an unknowing audience.

But then she notices that the middle-aged man is watching her. The Author. He's curious to see whether anyone will turn up, somebody she's been waiting for. A lover, perhaps? Or just a friend? How disappointed will she be? She understands that he's her cocreator in that moment. Or perhaps he's simply thinking: That girl has an aching back and finds it so embarrassing to stand while everyone else is sitting that she's pretending to wait for somebody, as if to tell them she's saved them a seat.

The next time she encounters him is down in the basement level of the student bookstore, where she once acquired all twelve volumes of *In Search of Lost Time*. He's giving a reading from his new novel. He catches sight of her—can't possibly recognize her after so many years—but it seems that he recognizes something about her all the same. Because he continues to seek out her gaze as he speaks about the book he's just written, as if it's her alone he wishes to address. Afterward, she asks him to sign the book containing the chapter she likes so much.

"To Rakel, with an especially strong wish that you will also read more of my work," he writes.

She sees him again outside the Platekompaniet record store in Stortingsgaten, where he's standing peering down into a bag of albums he's just bought. He looks uncertain. She wonders whether he's satisfied with his haul. Then he glances up, a far-off look in his eyes, and catches her looking at him. "We've seen you before," his eyes say. But before they can pass on the message to his brain, she slips past him and into the store.

"It's so strange—it's as if he notices me in some special way every time," says Rakel. "Without knowing that I'm the same person on each occasion."

"There's nothing strange about that," Jakob says. "Anybody with a good nose for these things can see straightaway that there's something special about you."

Then, in a thoughtful voice, he adds, "It's actually you he writes about in the short story that opens his debut collection. Because who else is the girl studying mathematics, the one the protagonist encounters in the cafeteria one spring day? The girl with flowing black hair, those soft curls, the lively eyes in a still face, the Mona Lisa smile? The girl so pure she won't sleep with him until they can be together forever—the most discerning example of the female sex he's ever met?

"You're also like the woman in his great romance novel—the woman the protagonist becomes obsessed with, whose deeply concentrating face never ceases to fascinate him. No wonder the poor author is astonished when he discovers that you actually exist in reality—that you're standing before him in person. That reality can surpass fiction. If you carry on like this, he'll end up having to write a book about an author who has written a novel in which he tries to prove that fiction is greater than reality, but who becomes disturbed by the fact that a woman who reminds him of one of his characters keeps popping up on his book tour, as if to prove that reality is greater than fiction after all!"

Rakel can't help but laugh. This is what she loves about Jakob. His riotous imagination. The ability to tickle her soul, in just the way that it needs to be tickled.

RAKEL HAS STARTED looking for mathematics conferences she can attend. Even though her illness makes traveling exhausting. She often gets so dizzy that she has to lie down—in airports, in university corridors, outside conference halls.

Moreover, she hates presenting her research results because there are always some middle-aged men in the room who insist on asking her questions afterward. Not because they're curious about her work, but in order to show off. To show that they know things that she probably doesn't. Always trying to force her into a corner, get the better of her.

They remind her of a student she had in her class the first time she taught a group of undergraduates. He was older than the others and didn't think Rakel had anything at all to teach him. After all, she looked younger than most of the students in the group. The man began to ask meaningless but impressive-sounding questions.

"But doesn't this go against the completeness principle?" he asked, in spite of the fact that the topic they were discussing had nothing at all to do with the completeness principle.

"No, it doesn't go against the completeness principle," said Rakel.

"Yes, it does," the man retorted.

"Then you'll have to explain why you think that," said Rakel.

"But it's obvious," said the man.

Rakel turned to the rest of the group. "Is anybody else wondering about this?" she asked. All the others shook their heads. "Then I think it might be better that we discuss it during the break," she said to the man.

But he continued to interrupt her every time she tried to explain an exercise. "But it goes against the completeness principle," he repeated. In the end, one of the other boys in the group turned to him and said, "No, it doesn't go against the completeness principle—are you a total idiot or something?" The man was quiet then, and after the break he disappeared from the group for good.

At conferences, there's nobody who knows her. Nobody to come to her aid and stand up for her.

But it's nice to go to conferences with Jakob. To be able to lie close to him all night, walk hand in hand with him through the streets. Jakob believes that it's impossible to really know a city before you've gotten lost in it. So when they arrive in a new town, they always make sure to get properly lost. It gives her such a warm, cozy feeling, to get lost with someone. To seek out the secret backstreets, to find the narrowest alleys and passageways.

But she would never have dared to get lost alone. She remembers the terror from when she was little and had to take the bus home from school on her own. When she still wasn't tall enough to pull the cord to alert the driver without clambering up onto her seat. But surely it wasn't permitted to stand on the seat with her shoes on. What if someone got angry at her?

Pappa said that she could just ask the bus driver to let her off at the right stop. Rakel had to ask Pappa what she should say. She practiced the sentences over and over again: "Excuse me. Could you please let me off at the stop closest to Kringstad road? I can't reach to pull the cord." She spent the entire journey afraid that the driver would forget to stop. That he would drop her off at a place where she didn't know where she was.

"DO YOU SEE that?" asks Rakel.

"See what?" says Jakob, setting his forehead against the window-pane in an attempt to peer inside.

He clearly sees only shelves full of bottles and boxes, and the advertisement that features a scantily clad woman with perfect skin and glossy hair.

"Have you really dragged me down here from the hotel just to show me this?" he asks. "You have your idiosyncrasies, but I wasn't aware you had a weakness for pharmacies."

"There," she says, pointing at the wall. "The painting."

It's an abstract color composition suggestive of a landscape. Shades of blue, with a curious, coarse structure—she can't tell whether it's layers of paint or pieces of fabric that have been painted into it. It's so beautiful that she had wanted to buy it immediately. But Jakob doesn't seem to understand why she's so captivated.

"Isn't it lovely?" she says. "It's just the kind of painting I've always wanted. Not smooth, but with resistance—and yet still so incredibly beautiful." She peers longingly into the crowded premises.

"Well, then, go in and take a proper look at it," says Jakob.

She looks at him, doubtful.

"You can just pretend to be looking for something to buy," he says.

She gives him another doubtful look and then slowly makes her way through the door. She walks back and forth alongside the shelves, pretending that she's perusing the products, casting the odd stolen glance up at the painting.

"You looked like a kid who had snuck into the adult section and thought you might get thrown out at any moment!" Jakob laughs when she comes back outside.

"It was even more beautiful than I thought," she says. "You go in— see for yourself." She almost pushes him through the doorway.

He repeats her maneuver, ostensibly browsing the shelves while occasionally letting his gaze glide over the painting.

She's almost jumping up and down when Jakob comes out again.

"Isn't it beautiful?" she says. "I wish I knew who painted it."

"Well, can't you just go in and ask?" The words slip out of him, and he seems to regret them immediately.

"Can't *you* do it?" she asks. "Your English is so much better than mine."

"Certainly not!" he says. "Your English is excellent, and at the very least more than good enough to have a conversation here in Portugal. And anyway, you're the one who knows what it is you want to find out."

"Can't you just ask who the artist is?" she says. "And whether he lives nearby?"

He shakes his head.

"Please," she says.

She doesn't often let herself use her eyes to beg. Maybe that's why it works every time.

Jakob goes back into the pharmacy and looks around. He's turned slightly green around the gills. She doesn't understand why she hates doing such things so intensely, but it's the same for him. When they travel to conferences abroad, they spend an inordinate amount of time and effort avoiding talking to people. The only difference between them is that she sometimes becomes so curious that she simply *has* to ask—if she can't dupe him into doing it, that is.

She stands and watches him through the window. He studies the shelves, then picks up a pair of nail scissors. He probably thinks his question will be better received if he buys something. There's a line at the counter, and he joins the back of it. She imagines him frantically practicing the little monologue he intends to perform.

The first person he encounters obviously can't speak a word of English, but disappears behind a curtain and returns with a man in a white coat trailing after him. Jakob asks his question again, and the man answers obligingly. Jakob gives a polite nod as he thanks the man for his help and pays for the nail scissors—and actually appears rather pleased with himself.

She's hopping from foot to foot when he comes back outside once more.

"You poor thing!" she says.

"It wasn't so bad," Jakob says, acting tough now it's all over.

"Your face turned green!" she says.

He shakes his head.

"But it did!" she insists. "Completely green! I always thought it was just a figure of speech, but it's actually entirely possible to turn green around the gills!" She laughs loudly.

He tells her what he's found out. The man in the white coat said the painting was likely by a friend of the owner, who often dropped in to exhibit his works. Unfortunately the owner wasn't there at the moment, but if they came back a little later in the week, the owner would surely be happy to help them.

Rakel enthusiastically declares that they have to come back another day.

· · ·

On the way back to the hotel she teasingly points out the green clothes she thinks would complement the new greenish cast to Jakob's complexion as they wander hand in hand down the main street.

But when they get back to the hotel room, she's suddenly sad. "To think that you were all green," she says. "It was awful of me to make you do that." She lies down on the bed, her face to the wall.

Jakob says it doesn't matter, but she curls herself up, her knees almost up to her chin. How could she do something like that to him? Why does she never learn to restrain herself?

SHE BECOMES MORE and more ill, has a constant sore throat, and develops food allergies that give her diarrhea and hives. She can no longer unscrew the lids of jam jars and drops everything she holds in her hands. If she overexerts herself, she gets a fever. It can rise to 102 at night, only to disappear again the next morning just as suddenly as it came. The important thing then is to lie completely still, so as not to overexert her body again.

She's developed a lump between her shoulder blades too. It's sensitive to heat and almost melts away when Jakob touches it. But then it grows, becoming large again by the next time he comes to visit her, and she has to ask him to put his hand between her shoulders once more. *Strumming my pain with his fingers.*

"So this is where the soul resides, between the shoulder blades," says Jakob. "They should have known, all those who think that humans don't have a soul. They must have neglected to look for it just there."

"The soul is only there when it clumps together," says Rakel.

"And where is it otherwise?" asks Jakob.

"Otherwise it's fluid, and much harder to locate," answers Rakel.

"Poor terrified little soul—we can give it a bit of heat treatment, so it can shift back into its fluid form," says Jakob. "But right now, I can at least kiss you, right on the soul."

Before he leaves her, she needs a weight transfer.

At first he thinks that this is something she's made up just to pro-long the visit, but when he understands that she really needs it, he stops protesting and lies obligingly on top of her, allowing all his weight to press down onto her.

"Here's some nice new weight for you," he says. "There."

She feels the impression of his body on hers long after he's left. This is the only way her body can feel itself. Otherwise, it would be weightless, shrivel up. His weight on her also makes the moment last longer, makes time pass more slowly. The way that in the universe time passes more slowly in the places where gravity is strongest. Especially in the vicinity of black holes.

DURING THE WORST spells, she goes to the Blue City to be cared for by Mamma and Pappa. She doesn't have the strength to prepare dinner for herself, never mind go to the store and buy groceries. But now and then she has better days, when she can take a walk to Kringstadsetra with Pappa. He pulls her up the steepest hills, almost like when she was a little girl. In her mind's eye, Rakel glimpses herself and Pappa walking through the quiet streets when she was small. Hand in hand. The days are so short and dark, but light shines from all the windows. No other people anywhere to be seen.

They walk down Kringstad road and cross the fields of Kringstad farm until they reach the forest trail that leads to Kringstadsetra. The darkness is spookier in the forest, but Pappa and Rakel sing in two-part harmony as they walk: "It Shines in Silent Villages." First Rakel sings the second voice while Pappa sings the higher first voice, and then they switch parts. Kringstadsetra lies there like a tiny revelation—just when they've been walking for so long that she's sure there will only ever be dark forest all around her. Then a plain opens up, and the trail leads to the steps in front of the little red cottage, where they sit down to eat the fresh rolls they've brought with them.

Rakel looks for constellations in the starry sky. The Plow, Orion's Belt, and Little Bear. Pappa says that the light from the stars takes a long, long time to reach earth. So when she looks up at the night sky, she's looking hundreds of years back in time. This makes Rakel dizzy. Because that means the light from the earth must also be out there, somewhere. Somewhere out there, at this moment, someone can now see Rakel being born. It's so nice that the light disperses in this way, that all of world history is somewhere out there in space.

On walks like this, Pappa would tell her how it's not only the musical tones that are oscillations. Light is also waves, and the short-wave, blue light oscillates the most, while the long-wave, red light travels along a straighter path. This is what makes the sky look blue, because the blue light scatters the most, out in all directions. And this is why rainbows are red on the outside and blue-violet on the inside.

But the strangest thing about colors is that they impersonate the opposite of what they are. Things that look blue reflect the blue light and absorb the other colors. So anything that looks blue is actually everything but blue. Blue is exactly what it isn't—it's the color it doesn't suck up, only what it throws out again.

And things that absorb all colors look black. Black carries all the colors within it, because it turns nothing away. Like black holes in space—the imprints of dead stars. Where gravity is so strong that it becomes impossible to escape once you've been caught. Then you'll be pulled into the black hole in a spiraling motion. Because gravity is so strong that even time itself is stretched out and passes more slowly in the vicinity of black holes.

RAKEL LIES IN the bed in her old childhood bedroom, feeling that life is unfair. She overdid it yesterday. She just never learns to adjust. But you have to allow yourself the indulgence of an experience every once in a while. Even if you have to pay for it afterward. Otherwise, life becomes meaningless.

How random everything is. That she ended up becoming a mathematician. That she fell ill. But also that she met Jakob. She lets her gaze slide across the wallpaper, with its pattern of yellow flowers. If Sofia Kovalevskaya had had such flowers on the walls when she was little, perhaps she might never have become a mathematician. Maybe she would have become an author instead? Maybe she would have been happier?

Sofia's interest in mathematics was piqued by a chance occurrence. When the house needed redecorating, the family had too little wallpaper, and so they covered the walls of the nursery with sheets of paper they found in the attic. These turned out to be Sofia's father's old notes from a course in mathematics he had taken in his youth.

Sofia was fascinated by the mystical symbols on the walls. She could stare at them for hours. The mathematics was too complex for her tutor to be able to help her with it, but Sofia was a precocious little girl. She decided to solve the mystery herself. She got hold of a math textbook, which she read in secret under her covers at night, because her father didn't think girls should be studying such things.

When Sofia was young, women were not allowed to attend university. So Sofia would probably never have become a mathematician if she hadn't met Weierstrass. But why had she stopped practicing mathematics for six years? After earning her doctorate in 1874, she moved back to Russia. She cut all contact with Weierstrass, stopped answering the letters he sent her, and started to become interested in literature instead. Did she become ill? Or was she perhaps suffering from a broken heart?

Jakob sends Rakel a text message that contains a link to the *xkcd* webcomic. The cartoon, titled "Angular Momentum," shows a girl spinning around and around next to a bed on which her boyfriend is sitting and watching her in amazement.

"What are you doing?" his speech bubble says.

"Spinning counterclockwise. Each turn robs the planet of angular momentum, slowing its spin the tiniest bit, lengthening the night, pushing back the dawn, giving me a little more time here, with you," answers the spinning girl.

Rakel is amused and sends Jakob a response: "Right now I'm spinning the other way, clockwise with the earth's rotation. All in the hope of making our planet turn the tiniest bit faster, so that time will pass more quickly and it won't be so long until I see you again."

"Cunning—you can spin both ways" is his answer.

ONE OF THE best things about mathematics, and part of what makes it like poetry, is that it opens new spaces for her. New spaces *inside* her. Abstract spaces. Spaces in higher dimensions. Infinite-dimensional spaces. Spaces where it is not necessarily possible to measure sizes and distances in the usual way. Before she started studying mathematics, she considered it a given that it is always possible to measure the distance between two points. But now she knows that this is only possible when one is in what mathematicians call metric spaces—spaces in which there is a distance measurement, what mathematicians call a metric.

Is there a human metric? Can a person be measured using letters and numbers? Rakel is in the university library, looking for an article about the construction of metrics in fractal spaces. She does an internet search using the term *metric*. Then she comes across a website called Humanmetrics. By answering seventy-two questions, she will receive a code that describes who she is. Four letters and four numbers in accordance with what is known as the Myers-Briggs Type Indicator.

She's always been a little skeptical of psychology, of the tendency to classify people and generalize from individuals, but today she's in the right mood to at least be entertained. So she answers the questions and is given the code to who she is: INFJ. I stands for Introvert, N for iNtuitive, F for Feeling, and J for Judging. Each letter is also assigned a number between 1 and 100 that specifies the extent to which she possesses the quality that the letter describes: I: 67, N: 62, F: 12, J: 67.

She'll have to test the system on other people. She sends Pappa the link to the website, and sees the results in black and white. He's a kindred spirit, only with a slight difference, a little twist: INTJ. Where she has an F for Feeling, he has a T for Thinking. "Crossing ferries" instead of "kissing ferries." But most surprising of all is that his numbers are exactly the same as hers. They are both introverted to exactly the same extent; they are also exactly as intuitive and exactly as analytical. Only in the quality that has the lowest value are they different. She ends up among those led by their emotions, Pappa among those who are led by their thoughts.

She has to try it on Jakob too. The next time she stops by his office, she gets him to take the test. He's INTJ too, only with different numbers. She's always known he's like Pappa. Jakob wants to know Rakel's code and begins to read the description of her personality type. He looks astonished as he reads:

> The rarest of all personality types. They often stand out, both in the complexity of their personality and in the extraordinary diversity and depth of their talents. They are often model students, who hold a special place in the hearts of their teachers. They attract others, but are often unaware of this themselves, since this is not something to which they ascribe importance. They have a strongly developed sense of morality and have a need to live by their moral convictions. They show such a great interest in other people and can seem so outgoing that they are often incorrectly assumed to be extroverts. But they have a truly introverted nature and are only able to be emotionally intimate with a few select friends and family members and with evident kindred spirits.
>
> They are the most poetic of all personality types and able to create beautiful and complex works of art. It is often easier

for them to express themselves in writing than verbally, and they are often excellent writers. They also have a radiant personality, which makes them well-suited to roles in which they can inspire others, such as teaching positions, especially within higher education, and the role of religious leaders. The professions of musician, author, and actor are also natural choices for this personality type. They are born psychologists, and perhaps the personality type most able to see through other people's hidden motives. But they might also be the personality type for which it is most difficult to make a clear career choice. Many of them feel inferior when encountering the hard logic of the sciences and therefore choose to study subjects within the humanities. But the small portion who choose a career within the technical sciences will achieve just as much success as their INTJ relatives, because it is their intuition—the dominant trait of the INFJ types—that gives them the ability to understand abstract theory and apply it in creative ways.

Jakob looks at Rakel. "This is you in a nutshell," he exclaims.

Rakel shakes her head. "Not everything fits," she says. "I don't attract other people."

"You have to read what comes after the comma too," Jakob says.

SHE HAS NEVER understood how to make friends. None of the children at school liked her. They teased her because of her dark hair and because of her name. None of the others were called Rakel. None of the others had dark hair like hers either. "O Rakel, oRacle, are you from Delphi?" they shouted.

It isn't me they're shouting at, she thought. They don't even know me. And nor will they ever get to know me.

Only her teachers liked her. Because she was such a good girl. She decided she'd make herself even better, so they would like her even more.

Jakob says that Rakel has to start letting other people in. "You're very open and intimate with me," he says. "How come you aren't like this with anyone else?"

"I only dare open myself up to people I know I can love infinitely," says Rakel, "so that I don't risk anyone loving me more than I can love them. But there are so few people I'm able to love."

"You must have been interested in boys other than me," says Jakob.

Rakel shakes her head. She didn't like any of the boys in her class. "Only the worst boys hung around me," she says. "The ones who threatened to beat me up if I didn't promise to marry them."

In kindergarten she had been engaged to three boys at once. Because she hadn't dared say no. It's such a long time until we grow up, they'll probably have forgotten it by then, she had comforted herself. But it was still a little scary all the same. Even though she had only kissed one of them—that time when they had climbed the rope ladder and he had spit loads of saliva into her mouth.

But then she remembers the boy with the blond curls. The one who was a couple of years older than her and much better at the violin. She'd been playing for almost three years, and had spent a week at a residential orchestra school with teachers from the Oslo Philharmonic and the Norwegian Academy of Music. They stayed in the dorms of an adult education college.

On the first morning at the residential school, Rakel wakes early to the sound of someone playing Bach. The very piece she's started practicing in secret—the Violin Concerto in A Minor. She tiptoes out into the corridor wearing only her nightgown and follows the sound. At the very end of the corridor is a little gathering place, with a sofa and large glass windows facing in both directions. And there he is. The boy with the blond curls. He looks out of the window as he plays. As if he wants to fill the whole world with Bach.

But then the boy catches sight of her and stops. "Did I wake you?" he says.

Rakel wants to say that it was the finest way imaginable to be woken up, but she only shakes her head. "I think I woke up because I'm hungry," she says.

"Breakfast isn't until eight o'clock," says the boy. "But I know how we can get something to eat anyway."

The front door is locked with a key, so they can't get out that way. But the boy takes her to his room and opens the window. He clambers up onto the windowsill and drops down onto the grass outside. When he sees how worried she is, he gestures to her, laughing.

"But we won't be able to get back in again if the door is locked," says Rakel.

"They open the door at quarter to eight—that's only half an hour from now," says the boy.

Rakel drops down onto the dewy grass too. And then she runs barefoot after the boy, up toward the main house where the teachers live.

"Wait here," he whispers. They've stopped outside a window on the ground floor, which stands ajar. The boy pulls himself up onto the window ledge and disappears in through the window. When he reappears, he's holding a packet of Marie biscuits and a cassette player. "I'll put it back again later, exactly where I found it," he says when he sees the expression on her face.

Then they sit down by the water and eat the biscuits. The boy turns on the cassette player. It's orchestral music. He turns up the volume. Rakel thinks it's the most beautiful piece she's ever heard. "What is it?" she asks.

"'Våren,' by Grieg," says the boy. "But I like the English name better. In English, the title isn't just 'Spring'—it's 'The Last Spring.'"

The next morning, she wakes to someone tapping gently at her door. Outside it, the boy is standing with the cassette player in one hand and a new packet of Marie biscuits in the other. "Did I wake you?" he says.

Rakel shakes her head.

"I thought you might be hungry today too," says the boy.

He opens the window and sits on the windowsill, his legs dangling outside. Rakel sits next to him. The scent of freshly mown grass rushes toward her, and Grieg's orchestral music fills her room with spring. From now on, she'll probably never be able to hear this music or eat Marie biscuits without thinking of the boy.

Rakel describes how, at the first music lesson yesterday, the professor from the National Academy of Music was horrified to discover that she never practices her scales.

"Scales don't have to be boring," says the boy. "Not if you improvise freely."

He picks up her violin to show her what he means. First, he starts with normal scales and triads, but soon he starts to twist them, playing them in new ways. He divides them into smaller chunks, inverts them, turns them upside down, lets major slide into minor. It's almost like listening to a piece by Bach.

Lastly, he shows her something she's never heard before—flageolets. He gently touches one of the strings with a finger, so that the fundamental note disappears and only the overtones can be heard. The sound is soft and flute-like. When he touches the string in the middle, the note is an octave higher, and when he touches the string a quarter way down its length, the note is two octaves higher. It's possible to play flageolets with two fingers too. He presses one finger down to shorten the string, while the other plays flageolets on the fourth and fifth.

"Have you started learning fractions at school?" the boy asks.

"Only just," says Rakel.

"Well, this is actually just mathematics," says the boy. He explains that the overtones work so well together with the fundamental note because the relationship between their frequencies is simple. The purest interval is the octave, because the one note oscillates twice as fast as the other, so that the relationship between their frequencies is one to two. Then comes the fifth, where the ratio is two to three. The fourth has a ratio of three to four, and so it goes on.

To think that fractions have always been a part of her life in this way. That she simply hadn't realized it, until now.

WHEN RAKEL WAS at school, she didn't know about any number systems other than whole numbers, rational numbers, and real numbers. But in her first year at university she learned about complex numbers. Which were given their geometric interpretation by mathematician Caspar Wessel—brother of the poet Johan Herman Wessel. While the real numbers sit all neat and proper along the x-axis, the complex numbers fill the entire plane. Some of the numbers are purely imaginary—they sit along the y-axis. But most numbers have both a real part and an imaginary part.

Rakel feels the most kinship with those that have a greater imaginary part than real part. She's always been fond of the little i because it's alone so much—and is itself both forward and backward. But the best thing about the i is that it's the imaginary unit, the square root of minus one. It's happier in unreality than it is in reality.

Every complex number has a complex conjugated twin, which is inverted—a mirror image—along the x-axis and has the same real part. Only the imaginary part is different: the equal-size opposite. If you multiply a complex number by itself, you get another complex number. But if you multiply a complex number by its complex conjugate, you get a real number.

So it's important to find your complex conjugated twin. And to multiply yourself by him—then the product will be real. Although you might find yourself having to wait eight years to do so.

ALTHOUGH RAKEL HAS no children, it's almost as if she has a little boy—the little boy from her neighborhood. She meets him one day when she's sitting on a bench outside the apartment block, reading *The Brothers Karamazov*.

When he's five months old, he twists himself away from his mother's breast because he'd rather look at Rakel. When he's one year old, he pulls up her sweater and crawls in under it. When he's two years old, he looks at her roguishly and says, "You're a girl. I'm a boy."

When he's three years old, he sits in the sandbox and says, "You don't have a house." Then he goes back to building his sandcastle and smiles. "But that doesn't matter. Because you can live with me."

When he's three and a half, he makes pink hearts out of Perler beads for her, even though blue is his favorite color. "Do you promise to take care of them?" he asks.

She nods.

"Forever?" he asks.

"Forever," she answers.

When he's four years old, he clambers up onto her lap and plays with her hair. "How come your hair is so dark?" he says, as he gently combs his fingers through it.

When he's four and a half, he presses his cheek to hers and asks whether she can teach him to count to one thousand. Both forward and backward.

When he's five years old, he moves to a place far away. And she thinks that this must be how a mother feels when she has to let go of her son. She will always be rooting for him, will cheer him on forever. One day, little man, you're going to make a girl very, very happy.

The most painful thing about not having children is not ever having tried. The fact that she has only herself to blame. She could have coped with fate not wanting to give her children. But can she live with never having tried? She pops into the maternity department of a clothing store and buys a pair of maternity pants, which she wears at home just to see how it feels. At least she manages to steer clear of the toy store this time.

In her mind's eye she sees a young woman buying a birthday present for the neighborhood boy. A young woman who feels so sad that she doesn't have a child of her own that she buys an extra birthday gift—for the child she hasn't had. She does the same the following year. And so her nonexistent child grows parallel to the boy from the neighborhood.

When he turns five, she finds a motorized carousel made of Legos. It's far too difficult for a five-year-old to build by himself, but with an adult to help out she's sure it'll be great fun. So she buys the merry-go-round for her nonexistent five-year-old and becomes so fascinated by the building techniques that she orders several more Lego sets. In the end she has quite the large collection.

"WHAT'S THE NICEST girl's name you can think of?" asks Rakel.

"Dunno," says Jakob.

"You don't know?"

"Rakel," he replies.

"Be serious," she says. "You didn't call either of your daughters Rakel."

"But I don't know! I've never thought about it," Jakob says.

"So how did your children get their names, then?"

"Well, I . . ."

"So what's the nicest girl's name you can think of?" she asks again.

"Ane, maybe. Or Ina."

"More!" she says.

"Irene . . . ?" says Jakob.

"Irene is old-fashioned," she says.

"What about you? Don't you have any names?" he asks.

"Ada and Iris," she replies.

"Any others?" asks Jakob.

"Siri, perhaps. But that's not quite as pretty, even though it's Iris backward."

"And Ada is herself backward," says Jakob.

"Smarty pants," she says. "But now we have to decide which ones we like best of all!"

. . .

She gets up and goes across to the drawer to get some paper and a couple of pens. Then she writes Ane, Ina, Irene, Ada, and Iris on a sheet, which she gives to Jakob.

"You have a hundred points to divide between these names. And I have the same."

She takes a piece of paper for herself too.

Jakob bends over his sheet of paper and concentrates on distributing the points.

"Done?" she asks.

"Yep," says Jakob, handing her his sheet.

He's given the most points to his own suggestions, but he's given quite a few to hers too. She starts to add up the points, and Jakob leans back on the sofa.

"We have a winner!" she says.

"So who is it?" asks Jakob.

"Ada, then Iris."

"Let me see!" he says, snatching her piece of paper from her.

She's given fifty points to Ada and fifty to Iris.

"That's cheating!" says Jakob. "You've only given points to the names you came up with."

"I said nothing about having to give points to all the names. And it isn't my fault that you didn't do your best to win."

"Okay, fine," says Jakob. "It doesn't really matter one way or the other, so if you want to win this game so badly, I gladly surrender."

"What about boys' names, then?" asks Rakel.

Jakob looks like he's starting to get tired of the game. "Arild," he says. "And Stian. What about you?"

"Sinus," she says.

"That's not a name!" says Jakob.

"Yes it is."

"Don't be silly."

"I can prove it," she says, moving over to the bookcase. She takes down the thick book of names she bought during the annual book sale and eagerly flicks through the pages. "Look, right here!"

"Sinus," reads Jakob. "Friendship, love, the core, the heart."

"Isn't it lovely?" she asks.

"Well, yes, but you can't call a child Sinus," replies Jakob.

"Why not?"

"There's nobody who is *actually* called Sinus."

"Yes there is—there's six of them! I've checked with the Office of National Statistics."

"Poor buggers," says Jakob.

"Let's vote!" she says.

He's seen though her strategy this time, and gives all his points to his favorite name. It's a tie between Sinus and Arild.

"You can't call a child Sinus," Jakob repeats. "Especially if you're a mathematician."

"We can call him Sindre Magnus and just use Sinus as a nickname, then," she suggests.

"Him?" says Jakob. "Him who?"

"Our son," she says. "If it's a boy."

He sighs. "You don't have the strength to look after a child—you can hardly take care of yourself."

She turns away. "You think I'm never going to get better?"

"Of course you're going to get better."

"Don't you want to have children with me?"

"Actually, I feel that I've had all the children I'm going to have."

"So what about me?" she says. "Will I never get to have a child?"

"I didn't say that. We'll see when you're well enough to take care of one."

. . .

If she gets well enough, he'll give her children. If it's a girl, she'll be called Ada. And if it's a boy, Sindre Magnus. And then they can call him Sinus for short. Ada and Sinus.

RAKEL HAS ALWAYS regarded Pappa as the best thing in her life—the single great joy that enables her to endure any and all pain. And the only person she can't live without. Pappa, who played tickling games with her at the piano. Pappa, who recorded her Aurora books onto tapes so she could listen to them over and over again. Pappa, who sat on the edge of her bed and sang to her when it was time to go to sleep:

> Darling Rakel, little one,
> come and put your hand in mine.
> No one in this whole wide world
> cares for you like I do.
> The love of the sun and the joy of living—
> if only I could always be giving
> all of this to my darling you,
> my dearest little girl.

Rakel thought the song was so sad. And what was so sad about it were the words "if only I could always be giving all of this to my darling you." Because "if only" denoted that this was a wish—that it wasn't possible in reality. He wouldn't always be there. And that thought was so unbearably sad. So she had to ask him to stop singing the song.

She had to ask him for other things too: "Remember to turn off the stove and the oven and to lock the door, and don't go anywhere this evening or during the night or in the early morning. And take Oskar away once I've fallen asleep." This last request was actually unnecessary—Pappa thought that Oskar took up too much space in the bed and that cuddly toys should sleep up on the shelf. But she said it so that Oskar could stay in bed with her until she fell asleep.

"Do you have to give me so much homework every night?" Pappa asked.

Rakel couldn't sleep without first ensuring she'd reminded him of everything, but after he'd said this, she'd just say, "Remember to do your homework!"

She once got so scared he was going to die that he ended up having to promise her that he'd live until he was seventy—just so that she could sleep at night. She'd worked out that she could then live safe and sound until she was thirty-seven years old. Inspired by a children's book she'd read about the life of Albert Schweitzer, she'd decided to divide her life into two parts. Up until the age of thirty-seven, she could be selfish and enjoy spending time on frivolities—like playing violin or doing mathematics. But then, when she lost Pappa, she would either have to find a worthy cause to die for or a worthy cause to live for.

She envisioned becoming an organ donor, because she thought that all she'd have to do was march into the hospital and say she wanted to donate all her organs. Then they'd let her pass away in her sleep and help themselves to the parts of her body they could use. The alternative was to become a mother in an SOS Children's Village in a poor country far away.

But what terrified her most of all was the idea that she might end up in heaven, while Pappa might end up in hell. At kindergarten, she'd been told that people who don't believe in God go to hell. And Pappa didn't believe in God. Which meant, of course, that he'd end up in hell.

But if Pappa didn't go to heaven, she didn't want to go to heaven either. Because she wanted to be wherever Pappa was. So she prayed a self-composed evening prayer: *"Dear God, I just want you to know that I don't believe in you. Please don't let Pappa end up in hell. If you send Pappa to hell, I want to go to hell too. But the fact that I'm praying to you for this doesn't mean that I believe in you. Just so you know."*

But she was unsure whether such a prayer would work in favor of its intended purpose or against it. She was also afraid that God—since she was praying to him—might conclude that she believed in him after all. And then perhaps he would send her to heaven, instead of to hell with Pappa.

Since Jakob came into her life, it feels—for the very first time—as if she might be able to live past the age of thirty-seven.

SHE FILLS THE years with Eva Cassidy's voice. "Fields of Gold." She fills them with R.E.M. "Everybody Hurts." She reads *To the Lighthouse* by Virginia Woolf and thinks it might be the most beautiful book she's ever read. Then she finds out that the author filled her pockets with stones and drowned herself. This happened on March 28, the very same date that Rakel first spoke to Jakob in the cafeteria. And she catches a glimpse of a little girl collecting stones in Kringstadbukta bay. Like a little Virginia Woolf with her pockets full of stones, she will always think hereafter.

She listens to Christian Ferras's interpretation of César Franck's Violin Sonata and thinks it might be the most beautiful interpretation of the piece she's ever heard. And then she learns that he too took his own life.

"The fact that you managed to complete your doctorate is quite simply a wonder, considering how ill you've been," says Jakob. "But you're able to do more running at just twenty percent capacity than the rest of us are able to do at our maximum. It just shows what potential there is within you, if only we could get you well."

Rakel has no idea how to get well, how to cope with working life. She doesn't have the strength to teach—she's so exhausted after two group sessions that she has to spend the rest of the week getting back on her feet. She feels bad for having accepted the research position at the university—she would never have been offered it had they known just how unwell she is. How little she gets done. That she mainly spends her time with her head on her desk, resting. One day, they're going to find out.

She can't help herself—she asks Jakob whether he's still sure. "It'll soon be eight years," she says. "Are you still sure you're going to choose me?"

"Of course," he answers. "Why do you ask? Are you feeling unsure yourself?"

Always this technique of turning things on their head, so that it seems as if everything is about her and her problems.

"But how can you bear to leave your family?" she asks.

"I'll finally be able to be with you," he answers.

"You'll have to help me develop a good relationship with your kids," she says.

"My son will be fine; it might be harder with the girls. But I'm sure we'll cope with that too," he says.

"We can live close by, so that they can still pop in whenever they like," she suggests.

He nods.

She doesn't understand how he can seem so unfazed. Is it because he isn't taking the situation seriously? Because he hasn't properly thought things through?

THE LAST SUMMER. Soon he'll leave his family. Soon they'll be together forever. It's about time—she is almost thirty-three years old. The text message he sends her while she's in the Blue City: "I'm reading Stein Mehren's love poems and thinking of you." She hears her favorite verse within her:

The light from a face that loves
forever opens out across the earth;
For the light in a face that loves
never ends—it is underway, always underway
in new people, in new lovers, timeless for all time.

Perhaps she should be hearing darker verses instead?

Will we then never quite leave each other?
Oh yes, we will always keep leaving each other.
Our end never quite ends. . . .
Oh this must be the deepest of solitudes.
To see one's solitude in the deep of a face estranged
and know: This face I once loved and opened
and chased to the darkness it came from.

She must try to be patient. Or try not to nag, at least. Even if there's something in his voice she doesn't quite understand. As if it's started to take on a slightly different tone, but not enough that she can put a finger on exactly what it is. He's unable to call her as often as he used to. It's so confusing. Why is he no longer able to do everything he managed to do before? She tries to hide how miserable she is, but ends up crying on the phone.

He says that he's just tired right now. He has a lot to do. "It'll be good for both of us to have a talk when you get back," he says.

HE MEETS HER on the platform. She's so happy to see him, wants to lie with her body pressed to his—right now, belly to belly. She doesn't understand why he's so eager for them to go to the store so she can buy groceries. They can do that afterward. He's acting oddly. But she lets him have his way.

"There's something I have to tell you," he says, once they've made it back to her apartment and put down the shopping bags. His voice is so serious that it frightens her. Has someone died? she wonders. One of his parents? Or has someone fallen ill? Oh, no—please don't let it be one of his kids!

"Lea knows about us," he says.

It takes a moment for her to understand who he's talking about, so rarely has she heard him say his wife's name. But that doesn't matter, she thinks, relieved—and is about to say that of course he can move in with her right away. It was going to happen in a few months' time anyway. In fact, maybe it's just as well that his wife has found out on her own. It might have been hard for him to make himself tell her.

"I have to end it with you, Rakel," she hears him say.

She looks at him in disbelief. Can't believe that he means it. Cannot comprehend how he could pronounce these words. She stares at his lips to see whether they can really have said the things she's just heard him say. It's suddenly so quiet. The music playing inside her has stopped. But then she hears a faint sound after all—the sound of something rupturing. She realizes that her skin has become too tight. She's no longer human, but an animal about to shed her hide.

Who is Jakob, really? And who is she? She hears her own voice blurt out a desperate *"No!"* Realizes that her mouth is open and that she should probably close it—if only she could remember how.

"But you don't love her," she says.

"I thought all my feelings were gone, but we've spoken so much lately that I've realized they're still there."

"But how can you suddenly love her again, just like that?"

"I've been reminded of all her good qualities."

"Such as?"

"Her magnanimity, for one thing. Many of the problems we've had have been my fault, because I got bored and lost interest. Now things between us are better than they have been for many years. And much of that is thanks to you, Rakel."

She tries to comprehend what he is saying. "Is it because I'm so ill? Because I've been away so much lately?" she asks.

He shakes his head.

She's sure that everything would have been different if only they hadn't been apart these last few weeks, if she hadn't been away when he made his decision. It feels so unfair that he hasn't included her in the process, that he hasn't kept her in the loop about the slightest thing. That he has planned to tell her this and simply vanish from her life—even though he's all she has.

"How could you let me wait so long for you if you don't love me?" she hears herself say. "We even chose names for our children."

"I don't know," he says quietly. "I don't know." And then, "I just wanted to lean your loneliness slowly against mine."

Lean your loneliness slowly against mine. Almost as in the poem by Stein Mehren. But Jakob said *slowly*—not *quietly.* Was this a mere slip of the tongue? Or, by exchanging these words, had he consciously captured the weight of their encounters—the weight that made time move more slowly and moments fix themselves forever?

I just wanted to lean your loneliness slowly against mine. What kind of excuse was that? It was hardly a tenable explanation. He was obviously still just as full of poetry and bullshit as ever.

"You say the strangest things when you're drunk," she used to say to him.

"I haven't touched a drop of wine all day," he'd said to her—a little insulted—the first time.

"You say the strangest things when you're drunk," she'd repeated. "Drunk on life, drunk on lust—intoxicated by love."

Can gold be turned to granite with nothing but words? Can happy moments turn unhappy when looking back on them from the future? He'd once asked her about this. "After people get divorced, many of them seem to think that everything was shit all the time," he'd said. Her response back then had been: "Even if they see things that way from some point in the future, that doesn't change the fact that they felt happy there and then."

But his words have changed her from gold to granite in an instant. She can no longer imagine that she's made of precious metal, that she's suffered for the benefit of others. Now she is only granite. No, worse than that. She's nothing but the muck beneath the stone. A common mistress. Not the great love of his life, as he had led her to believe.

That night she goes out onto her eighth-floor balcony and sits on the railing with her legs hanging over the side. Right now, she doesn't give a damn about the poor bastard who'll have to find her. Right now, she can't take any more. She looks out across the sleeping city. Gray clouds, but no rain. No stars in the night sky. No tears either. In the east, the sky has already started to brighten. When the city wakes, she'll no longer exist.

Then she catches sight of it—a rainbow over Nesoddtangen. In the exact same place she's so often fixed her gaze and thought about Jakob at home with his family. A rainbow, right when she needs it most. No sun in sight. No raindrops either. So then how is it possible for a rainbow to appear? It stretches straight up toward the sky, like a deprecating hand. *You simply cannot do this, Rakel. No one will ever be able to forgive you for it.*

THE NEXT MORNING, she finds a message from Jakob on her phone. He writes that he's so worried about her. If she wants to, they can meet and talk things through.

She wants to. She wants to win him back.

"Have you told your wife everything?" she asks.

"She didn't want to know how long it's been going on for. I just said it's been going on for a long time."

"But can she forgive you, just like that?"

"She's said she'll try to forgive me this time. I've never done anything like this before, after all. But any more messing around, and I'll be straight out the door."

"And yet you've come here?" she says.

"I can't lose you as a friend. I've told Lea that I need to be able to keep seeing you, and she knows that I'm here with you now."

How magnanimous she is, thinks Rakel. I almost wish I could offer her an apology.

Then the sobbing breaks over her, her entire body shaking with it.

"What is it, Rakel?" he asks.

"I don't know if I can bear to be just friends with you. I don't know what we can do together anymore."

"We can do almost everything," he says.

"But I'm going to miss lying close to you—belly to belly—so much." He sighs.

"You can lie close to me, dear friend. Come here."

So they lie in her bed, belly to belly, and she can feel just how much his body desires to make love to her, even though his head says no. He lies there like a huge self-contradiction. She thinks that this is a somewhat peculiar interpretation of the term "friendship," and probably not the type of friendship that his wife has in mind. But Lea has said that if he gets himself mixed up in anything else, then he'll be straight out the door.

And that means if she can just get him mixed up in something, he'll be hers. She needs to know that he really means it's over between them at any rate. She presses her lips to his and notes with satisfaction that he can't resist kissing them. Then she lies on top of him, and even though she can see that he doesn't want it—not with his head, anyway—she lowers herself onto the stiffness of him.

This is how it is to rape a consenting man. She sees the despair in his eyes at what he's about to do. At the fact that he can't even keep his promise for a single day.

"Like this," she whispers in his ear. "It goes in here. It can hurt a little the first time. After that, it gets better."

Then he can no longer resist her and thrusts himself deep inside her, making love to her with a passion so sincere it makes her sure it isn't over.

"You love me," she says.

"Yes, I love you," he says. "That's the problem."

THE NEXT DAY, Jakob is the one who takes the initiative. She was obviously right when she said it only hurts the first time. Once you've committed that first sin, you may as well keep sinning. But for her, something has changed.

"You have to decide which one of us you want," she says. "At least, we can't keep on like this. I feel so guilty toward *her*. I'll help you stand by your decision, no matter who you choose. But I have to be sure of what you want."

He doesn't know what he wants, is unable to choose. She sees the distress in his face.

"You can have a year," she says. "But I have to have an answer within a year—and preferably as quickly as possible. As soon as you're sure."

DEAR RAKEL, YOU *have excellent taste in problems.* To think that these were the first words he wrote to her. If only they had known it back then, just how right he would turn out to be.

As she walks through the student housing area with its red brick buildings, she imagines a young girl sitting on the lawn outside her new student room, lost in a book she's been given as a parting gift by the high-school teacher she's so fond of. A young girl who has no idea just how thoroughly she will one day make the book's words her own: *Love is the origin of the world and its ruler, but all its ways are filled with flowers and blood, flowers and blood.*

But why does she feel so ashamed? And what is shame, really? She finds the following definition in a book: "*Shame is the intensely painful feeling or experience of believing that we are flawed and therefore unworthy of love and belonging. It's the fear that something we've done or failed to do, an ideal that we've not lived up to, or a goal that we've not accomplished, makes us unworthy of connection.*"

The author writes that the secret lies in regarding one's own vulnerability as a strength. As the basis for all love and empathy, as the very fabric from which true compassion is created. The difference between happy people and unhappy people is that the former believe they deserve to be happy, and to be loved.

But what use are definitions and secrets when she doesn't know what to do with them? She still doesn't know how she's going to venture out into the world of others, where love and forgiveness can be found. Where she just might learn to forgive herself. She needs some benevolent people in her life, people who won't turn away when they discover what she has done. Who she really is.

The only person who has always been there for her is Pappa. Pappa, who linked the world together for her. Who showed her that there are just a few basic principles that recur everywhere—making the sky blue and enabling rainbows to appear. She closes her eyes. Pappa is on his knees on the road beside her. They're studying mirages—a kind of practical joke on nature's part—that make Rakel see something that isn't really there. It looks as if there is water on the asphalt, even though it's completely dry.

Pappa explains that this is because the warm air just above the ground reflects rays of light, just as they are reflected by the surface of a body of water. So it looks as if the road is reflecting the sky in the same way that the fjord does. That's why it looks like water. The refraction of light is also what makes her finger look broken when she sticks it into water. And if she lies underwater and looks straight up at the sky, she will see only a circular disk of light where the rays from above penetrate the water's surface, while everything beyond it is dark.

IMAGINE IF JAKOB is actually the kind of person who uses his students. Who uses his position to obtain sexual favors at work—and all while being paid to be there. It's a fucking cushy deal, if so. She has seen it herself, the way his head turns after the girls in the department. How eager they are to greet him in the elevator, the way they continually drop by his office. And how he casually increases his speed when a girl with a promising bottom walks past—obviously in order to be able to examine said bottom more closely, and to classify it by firmness and shape. She's hardly the first person he's made a pass at.

Perhaps if she takes a temporary position at Statistics Norway, she might find answers to some of the things she's been wondering about. "Yes, good day. I'm calling from Statistics Norway. We're conducting a survey about the population's sexual habits. May I please speak with the member of the household with the first upcoming birthday who is a married or cohabiting partner and who is over twenty years of age? Question 1: How often do you have sex with your spouse/partner? Question 2: How many sexual partners have you had in the last eight years?"

But if Jakob answers the phone, he'll recognize her voice. She refuses to stoop so low, and casts the thought aside.

Instead, she forces herself to remember the pain. The pain of being continually forsaken. How easy it is for him to abandon her, to simply shut her out of his life whenever it suits him. Which means that the good can never just be good—that it always hurts at the same time.

Like the first time they had sex. They were away at a seminar with the rest of their department, and when they went down to breakfast afterward, he acted as if he hardly knew her, even though everyone knew he was her supervisor. He talked enthusiastically with everyone but her, and on the bus back to the university he sat next to the flirtatious office assistant. Rakel didn't even get to say goodbye to him, even though she would be leaving for the Blue City that very afternoon. And after he had visited Rakel to tell her it was over, he had gone straight out to a café with a female former student.

But then it isn't all or nothing. It's a mixed bag, a mixed blessing. She glimpses a young woman lying belly to belly with her best friend. He's a middle-aged man. They've found a remote bay at Gressholmen and have just been swimming in the sea. Now they're lying on the smooth coastal rock, letting the sun warm their salty bodies. The tall reeds conceal them.

She feels the gnawing ache in her lower abdomen that makes her forget good intentions and guilty conscience, forget everything but the hungering for him to fill her completely. The longing to feel him so deep inside her that the universe contracts into a single, glowing point before exploding in waves of heat that spread through her entire body. To feel the birth of the universe inside her. The Big Bang. It's irresistible.

Trying to resist the best of what life has to offer is futile. Such moments are worth all the pain in the world. She cannot live without them. Because even though there's mostly granite, the gold shines more brightly.

THE OLD POET—the woman who wrote the most beautiful love story of the century. Who fell for a much older author while he was still married and waited several years for him to be hers, only to discover that he was a selfish drunk and wife beater. In addition to being a brilliant and gifted author. Rakel encounters her on the steps outside the Nansen Academy during the Norwegian Festival of Literature in Lillehammer. She's just heard the woman give a talk about her life, about how her stormy relationship with her husband and the trivialities of her familial duties prevented her from writing. Rakel wonders whether the woman believes she would have written better had she made different choices. Whether it might be necessary to choose between love and writing great literature.

"Excuse me. I heard you speaking about your life and how your difficult marriage prevented you from writing, how it became a kind of competition between the two of you. But your relationship with him was also what gave you the material for some of your best work. So I wondered, as you look back on it now, what advice you might give to the young author you used to be? Would you advise her to choose differently?"

Rakel is suddenly horrified at the personal question she has heard herself ask and hurries to add, "You see, I just read a book about a young author who wonders whether she has to choose between love and writing great literature. And I'd love to hear your thoughts on that."

A surprised smile slips across the old woman's face, as if she's being asked to consider life from a new perspective. Her expression lights up with such a friendly pensiveness that Rakel immediately feels a fondness for her.

"You know, when you encounter such a great love, you can't help but follow it," the woman says eventually. Rakel thinks this is the greatest comfort she could have wished for.

The next day, Rakel sits at the back of the room and listens to the old poet read from the poetry collection she likes best of all. She studies the fine lines on the old woman's face, the wise but simultaneously childlike expression between all the wrinkles. And she hopes that she will age in the same way one day.

When the audience erupts into applause, the woman lifts her gaze and looks out across the gathered crowd. The sunlight pierces the window and hits Rakel just as the reading ends, and perhaps this is why the old woman catches sight of Rakel, letting her eyes rest on her face in recognition. As if she is studying Rakel's features too, with a strange sense of catching a glimpse of her younger self.

"YOU'RE AN EVEN sorer loser than I thought," says Jakob. "You're red in the face with frustration!"

He seems amused. She made a huge mistake toward the end of the game, practically handing him the victory on a plate. They always play for a small prize. She likes to save up her prizes for later—she's owed fifty-four so far.

But now that Jakob has finally won a prize, he wants it straight-away. And he seems to be relishing making her give it to him while her cheeks are still burning.

"You win over ninety percent of the time," he says. "Not only are you a much better player than me, but you concentrate much harder too. I often end up so enthralled at just watching you concentrate that I forget to follow the game. While I'm busy collecting points using the strategy you employed last time, you've already come up with some-thing new and end up winning anyway. So surely you can't begrudge me a single prize?"

"So what do you want for your prize, then?" Rakel asks.

"I want to hear you play piano," says Jakob. "You never touch the old piano you inherited from your grandmother."

Rakel hesitates. The piano is not her instrument, and she's com-pletely out of practice. She hasn't played in over twenty years. But Jakob insists that this is the only prize he wants, and he wants it now. She sits down on the stool and wonders whether her fingers will remember anything at all. She decides to try Debussy. One of the last pieces she played—"Arabesque."

She plays from memory, and messes up several of the runs. At certain points she blanks out completely, and has to start again. She shakes her head in defeat. But after a while it gets easier. Her fingers remember where they need to go, and she can disappear into the music. But then the notes clash again. Finally, she manages to make it through the entire piece.

She turns to Jakob. "You see," she says. "I can hardly remember anything. It's just a mess."

But Jakob claps enthusiastically. "I suddenly have a better understanding of what it means to be musically gifted," he says. "There was something about the way you played that truly affected me—the sensitivity, your touch, or the variations in tempo and strength."

"But I made so many mistakes," says Rakel.

"But for me, having never heard the piece before, I think that might have been an advantage," says Jakob. "The fact that you had to go searching made it easier for me to understand what you were looking for."

JAMES JOYCE WATCHES over them when they make love. With his broad, virile stance, hands deep in his trouser pockets and head cocked to one side, he watches them. He never says anything. Always keeps a straight face, never doffs his cap in salutation. Still, she gets the impression he likes what he sees.

Sometimes she gets the strange feeling that he's writing about them. If she ever has a serious crack at *Finnegans Wake*, perhaps she'll find the two of them there, in a book written long before they were born. It'll be the details that give them away. All her little quirks. The backs of the knees, the toes, the nape of the neck, the ears. How many people actually lose all self-control at having a tongue stuck in their ear? Or all his flights of whimsy afterward. The Beatles songs he drums on her naked bottom. Or his astoundingly successful attempts to prove that any text can be sung to the melody to "Vårsøg." And occasionally something they didn't know will be written there, but will appear so apt that they simply have to concede: "Yes, this is us!"

She's set a copy of *Ulysses* in front of the other books in the bookcase, its cover facing outward. And there he stands. With his hands deep in his trouser pockets and his head cocked to one side. She placed the book there like that because she's borrowed it from Jakob and doesn't want to forget to give it back. But he's told her to keep it, says it belongs up there on the shelf. Like an eternal monument to all it has seen.

"WHAT ABOUT MY prize?" asks Rakel.

"Yes, what about it?" replies Jakob.

"I want it now," she says.

"Here?" he says, casting a quick glance at the people around them. "Wouldn't it be better to wait until we're alone?"

"They won't hear us. The plane's engine is too loud," she says.

For a moment he looks at her as if he thinks she wants to cash in her prize by slipping off her underwear beneath her summer dress, straddling him, and taking him right there and then. But she isn't *that* crazy. Although the time she took off all her clothes and stood naked outdoors in October, despite the fact that it was only forty degrees outside, probably surprised him. It was still light enough that her skin shone pale in the dusk. Any passerby would have seen them, and the thought had apparently made it impossible for him to penetrate her.

"Okay," he says. "What do you want to use your prize on?"

"I want to exchange it for ten questions."

"*Ten* questions? You really think you deserve *ten* questions for beating me at Othello?"

"Okay, three questions then. But you have to answer them truthfully—and if you don't answer them in enough detail, I'm allowed to ask follow-up questions."

"And who gets to decide what's enough detail?" he asks.

"I do," she says. "But I'm only allowed to ask one follow-up question per subject."

"So now you've suddenly gotten yourself six questions instead of three?" he says.

"Are you ready?" she asks.

"I doubt it, but it doesn't seem that I have any choice."

"Buckle up!" she teases.

He's already sitting there with his airplane seat belt fastened.

"What are the ten things in your life that you're most ashamed of?" she asks.

"That's cheating!" he says. "You can't ask about ten things—to do that you'd have to ask ten questions."

"But I only asked one," she replies. "You have to answer."

He seems to be struggling to find something appropriate to say. "I used to feel ashamed that I was attracted to boys as a teenager."

"But that's nothing to feel ashamed about," she says.

"And I'm ashamed that giving girls a good spanking turns me on," he says, giving her an eager look.

"So that's what you're doing in secret in your office?" is all she says with a cheery smile. She hopes he'll drop this line of thinking, but it seems it's too late to stop him now.

"And I'm ashamed that I get aroused at the thought of being spanked myself."

"Well, that's not anything to feel ashamed about either," she says.

He looks at her as if she doesn't understand anything in the slightest.

"That was three things, you still have seven left," she says.

"I can't think of anything else off the top of my head."

"Well, if you think of something, you have to tell me later."

"Next question?" he says.

. . .

"How many girls have you slept with?"

"Not that many," he says.

"That's not a proper answer."

He avoids meeting her gaze.

"Then let me ask you a follow-up question. What are the names of the girls you've slept with?"

"That is in no way a follow-up question," he says. "That's worse than the first question you asked."

"That's what happens when you don't answer with enough detail."

"I don't want to expose my former lovers to you," he says. "How would you feel, if I were to share the details of my relationship with you with another lover?"

She stares at him. "Do you intend to take lovers other than me?"

"Oh, I give up!" he says.

"But you haven't answered my question yet."

"Knock it off!" he says.

"But this is my prize! Fine, you don't have to say their entire names. Just the first letters."

"J, L, H, G, C, E, K, R," he says.

"You've slept with *eight* people?" she says.

He clearly thinks this isn't so many for a man of his age. "No, only three," he says. "That's a list of everyone I've ever been in love with."

"I've only ever been in love with you," she says. "How many of the women on your list have been your students?"

"All except two. But now I think you've long since used up all your questions."

"That was just a follow-up question because you answered so poorly," she says.

"Okay, but now you only have one question left," he says.

"How often do you sleep with your wife?" She notices that a crack has appeared in her voice.

"That has nothing to do with you! Surely I'm allowed to sleep with my own wife," he says. He looks as if he wants to slap her.

"Yes, of course you are—but then what are you doing with *me?*"

"I don't think it's right to ask people questions like that. It's reminiscent of an interrogation. People have a right to keep certain things to themselves. And now you've crossed the line."

"I never would have asked if we were together, just the two of us," she says. "You must understand that it's different when I have to tolerate you sleeping with her at the same time. I need to know more in order to feel safe."

"Twice a week," he says.

She blinks away the tears.

"Well, you wanted to know," he says. "If you can't handle hearing the truth, perhaps you should stop pestering people for it."

"Do you still think you're going to choose me?" she asks.

"Well, I'm certainly not becoming any surer of it with you carrying on like this!" he says.

She turns to face the window. Hopes she hasn't ruined everything, hopes he isn't tired of her. He's told her that she has a unique ability to turn anything positive into something negative. They've just spent a week together in Copenhagen—she'd been pestering him for it for ages. Not only to be able to sleep with him, but to *sleep* with him. There's a difference. He doesn't understand how painful it is for her every time he leaves her, how she misses him when he isn't around. But it's best not to say any more.

She sits there, looking at the city that stretches out like a Sierpinski carpet below them. The pattern slowly becomes more detailed, streets, parks, and buildings appearing as the plane prepares to land. The sun has left a strip of rust across the sky.

They leave the plane in silence. Jakob doesn't even comment on the fact that her shoelaces have come undone. He simply hurries on as she bends down to tie them.

. . .

When they've collected their baggage, she can't help but say something regardless. "Can I ask for something for my birthday?"

He looks at her, surprised. Probably because she doesn't usually concern herself with material things. This is in fact what he's said he likes about traveling with her, that shopping is never at the top of the list of things she wants to do.

"Your birthday is still weeks away," he says.

"The only thing I want for my birthday is for you not to sleep with your wife. Just for that day."

RAKEL LIES IN bed, listening to the radio. It's violin music, "Melodie" by Gluck. From the opera about Orpheus and Eurydice. The piece she used to listen to Arthur Grumiaux playing on the record player when she was little, back when she still didn't understand how Orpheus could be so stupid as to turn around too soon.

She didn't catch the name of the violinist, simply lies there listening to the colors in his tone. The lyrical timbre causes something to vibrate within her, makes her want to laugh and cry at the same time. His melancholy is deeper than Grumiaux's. It's as if she can hear both the love and the pain at losing one's beloved forever.

She fetches her shoes and sets them on the bed. If she becomes good at tying her shoelaces, perhaps Jakob will like her better. He always gets irritated when her laces come undone. At first, he thought it was charming. But as they say, most of what seems charming eventually starts to get on one's nerves.

She experiments with different variants. She starts with a simple knot at the bottom by crossing the left lace over the right and twisting it down behind and forward again with her index finger. Then she creates a loop on the left lace. If she feeds the right lace around from behind and creates a loop through the hole from the front, as she usually does, the knot will be weak. But if she instead feeds the right lace around from the front and creates a loop through the hole from behind, the knot will be strong. She wonders whether Jakob will notice how she's improved.

She takes out the book she bought online, *The Ashley Book of Knots*. It contains four thousand of them. She becomes so fascinated by the art of tying knots that she teaches herself five new knots per day—there's no telling when she might need them. Reef knot. Sheet bend. Bowline, timber hitch, sheepshank, half hitch, clove hitch, double fisherman's knot, slip knot. She teaches herself a magic trick too, an "elusive knot," where she starts with two half hitches and lets the last two knots modify the first two. But what's the use in her being a knot-theory whiz kid when she's faced with the knots in the thread that connects her to Jakob?

SOON A YEAR will have passed. A year in which her chronology has been reversed. In which she has counted down, toward the moment he will determine her future. Four weeks remaining. Three weeks. Two. She doesn't know whether she wants time to move quickly or slowly. The waiting is insufferable, but on the other hand this might be the last period of time she's able to spend with him.

When she asks Jakob whether he's decided, he answers that he'll never let her go again. "I just can't do it," he says.

Still, there's nothing to indicate that he's planning on leaving his family. And so you're leaving the hardest part to me, she thinks. Forcing *me* to be the one to leave you. Because she knows now that he'd prefer to stay with his family. If only he had the willpower to resist her.

So she forces it out of him. Says that if he doesn't leave his family by a given date, it's over. Clings to the hope that he will choose her for as long as she can. Is proud of herself for having resisted the temptation to tell Lea just how thoroughly she's been duped this past year. That no more than a month ago, Jakob was with Rakel in Copenhagen, that week he said he was at a mathematics conference. That they lay in the park under a great tree, looking up at the stars as the darkness enveloped them. And that Jakob fulfilled one of her greatest wishes—to be made love to outdoors under the starry sky.

But that's not the way she wants to win him. She doesn't want him if he doesn't choose her. And he doesn't. Despite the fact that the date contains both her lucky and her favorite number. She lies curled up on the bed when he leaves.

Now you've lost everything, Rakel. Your health. Your work. The one you love above all others. Pappa and Mamma are all you have left. And you think they would be so ashamed of you, should they ever learn of this, that it would be easier for them to handle their grief if you simply died in an accident. But if you die now, Rakel, all you will leave behind are a few letters and numbers:

Rakel Havberg: August 19, 1974–August 19, 2008

And your life will have been nothing but that brief line between the digits. It might be hard to find a date of death that looks more beautiful next to your date of birth. But you must leave a little more behind you. You must leave a few more letters yet.

HER CHILDHOOD BEDROOM is almost exactly as it was in the old days. But Pappa has purchased a hospital bed, so she can raise the head end during the day. And Mamma has sewn new curtains, to help her sleep better at night. She spends almost all day in bed, only getting up for brief spells before she's drained of all strength and has to lie down again. Before, she had her hours with Jakob to look forward to, something to think about other than the illness. Now she no longer has a future. She's going to be alone for the rest of her life, because it's impossible to meet new people when you have to lie under the covers all day.

Jakob continues to send her limericks on her phone every single evening. It hurts so much that she has to forbid him from getting in touch with her. "Please leave me alone," she writes. "If you love me, you have to let go of me now. Otherwise I'm afraid I'll disappear down into a black hole forever." But then she regrets it. Hopes his reply will be that he can never let her go, that he regrets the choice he has made. That he finally understands he cannot live without her.

But no reply comes. She checks her phone as soon as she wakes, and every hour until she goes to sleep. What if he's ill? What if he dies before she can see him again? Then it'll be too late. Then she'll have to regret this for the rest of her life.

Fuck him and his ability to carry on as if nothing has happened. With strength enough to give his lectures and the energy to write limericks. To go to cafés with his female students. Play the role of father, sleep with his wife, and find himself new lovers. While Rakel can't even be in the same city as him—she wouldn't be able to resist the urge to seek him out, would do anything just to be able to see him. End up begging him to let them continue as before.

On the top shelf is Oskar, just like when she was little. And on the shelf below are all the ring binders containing her school exercise books. But then she catches sight of something she'd forgotten. The book she was given by Miss on the last day of school, because Miss was sure that Rakel was going to be an author. The pages of the book have gilt edges and the cover is bound in leather; it looks like a Bible. But the pages are blank, and must be filled by Rakel. On the first page is her name, written in gold script. It was David who wrote it.

"Rakel Havberg," he'd said, satisfied. "If you ever want to publish what you write, you can use a pseudonym."

"Why?" Rakel wanted to know.

"So that you'll be freer not only to get closer to yourself, but also to become someone you've never been," David had answered. "You can use the letters of your name, the same building blocks, just in a different order. Like another chance. Someone you might have been if only you had made different choices. What about Vera H. Kalberg? Klara H. Bergve? Or perhaps Brage H. Raklev?"

Inside the book is a letter, enclosed by Miss, with a statement from a real author:

> I have had the pleasure of perusing a collection of poems by Rakel Havberg. I am struggling to overcome my consternation at the fact that such a young author is able to write in such a fresh, vivid, and inspired way. Several of the poems make me think of Inger Hagerup, but I have a sneaking suspicion that Rakel Havberg has no need of any great role model. Even now, at her

young age, she is already writing with a strong and personal literary voice. Who knows what greatness awaits her?

But most of all, Rakel remembers the following lines: "You are going to feel the need to write, but let it come when it must. Do something else first."

Is now the time for her to start writing? She's struggling to feel any great urge. All she ever manages to get down on paper are disjointed fragments of text, almost like keywords. She can only write a couple of lines a day. Something about black holes. Gravity. Time. In search of lost time. Sofia Kovalevskaya. Stein Mehren. Wonderful. She has promised Jakob never to speak of their relationship to anyone. But she has never promised not to write about it. She imagines a suitable insult for her novel's dedication:

For Jakob. Here is a novel in which the heroine is greater than me, and the antihero smaller than you.

She imagines the book reviews too. And a place in Edvard Beyer's *History of Literature*. "The most beautiful literary portrait of a woman since Kristin Lavransdatter." Or: "An innovative novel, and a precursor to *The Fragmented Structuralism*." Or, best of all: "With this book on my nightstand, I feel less alone."

But she doesn't even manage to finish the novel's opening.

PERHAPS SHE SHOULD have started with something easier first. It isn't a bad idea to have written a short story before making a start on an entire novel. But she's never liked practicing anything other than what she actually wants to do. It's like scales on the violin. Instead of doing them, she just made a start on the pieces she wanted to play and learned what she needed as she went along.

It was the same with mathematics. She always had to start with a problem she was interested in solving; any theory she needed she learned along the way. She's never been able to just sit down and read a mathematics textbook from A to Z, because she needs to see things in the right frame of reference. Context plays a role.

A typical writing exercise in Norwegian class at school was to create a sentence containing a metaphor for the moon: "The moon is a . . ." And they were supposed to fill in the blank with an appropriate image, preferably something more original than "yellow cheese." But this kind of thing is meaningless to Rakel, because what's appropriate depends on the overall situation. On what the sum of the past and the present is at precisely this point. It's the surrounding context that tells her what the moon is like.

The secret is not to simply present the images that come to her; she must present them through someone's eyes. The light must be refracted by someone in such a way that it says something about the person it is refracted through. Just as the light's angle of refraction when transitioning from one medium to another says something about the material through which the light passes, about its density. The law of the angle of incidence and the angle of refraction. The way light is always refracted toward the normal line when it passes into a medium with greater density.

SHE RAISES THE head end of the bed and lies there, looking at the children's books that still line the bookcase. The Aurora books by Anne-Cath. Vestly, and those about Guro, who plays violin in an orchestra. Aurora and Guro were her best friends. And David, of course, even though she had made him up herself. She found him on the cover of a book Mamma gave her.

She had just experienced her first tragedy, losing her grip on the string of the yellow balloon Pappa had given her during the Constitution Day celebrations. She stood there, watching it disappear up toward the sky, a dying sun that became smaller and smaller until not even the tiniest dot of it remained in all the blue.

After she had grieved for the balloon for three days, Mamma had brought her the book. On its cover was a picture of a girl in a blue dress with a boy standing right beside her. The boy was holding the string of a balloon, and the girl was excitedly stretching her arms toward it. Rakel understood that the boy was sharing the balloon with the girl because she had lost her own. He was probably either her big brother or her best friend. She called him David.

Her eyes slide across the wallpaper with its yellow flowers and stop at the only poster on the wall. Mamma gave it to her. It's an image of a bird in free flight, and beneath it are the words:

If you love something, set it free.
If it comes back to you, it's yours forever.
If it doesn't, then it was never meant to be.

Mamma came home with a baby rabbit—just the kind that Rakel had wished for. When she let it out of the box, it hopped under the kitchen counter and huddled in the farthest corner. Its entire white coat was trembling. Rakel understood that she had to be patient. She sat down on the floor and waited. "I know that you miss your mamma," she whispered. "But I'm going to take good care of you, always. We're going to be very good friends, you and I."

When she came home from school, Hoppsasa would come bounding toward her. Rakel would lift the rabbit up onto her lap and open her mouth as wide as she could, and Hoppsasa would stick her snout into Rakel's mouth. It was their secret greeting. If Rakel was sad, she burrowed her face into Hoppsasa's soft fur, and the rabbit would lick her hand with its rough, warm tongue. But if Rakel was happy, Hoppsasa jumped teasingly around the veranda and was impossible to catch. It was almost as if they were playing tag. First Rakel would run after Hoppsasa and try to catch her, and then Hoppsasa would run after Rakel and nudge her feet.

But one day Pappa said that it wasn't good for a rabbit to live in captivity, even if it got to hop around freely on the veranda. "You can see how Hoppsasa is leaving bitemarks in the railing," he said. And Rakel understood that it was better for Hoppsasa to live in freedom.

So she and Pappa took Hoppsasa out into the forest. At first, Hoppsasa sat completely still. But then she hopped away across the heath, cautiously at first and then with wild, bounding leaps, farther and farther away, until she disappeared into a blueberry patch. Rakel was pleased that Hoppsasa was happy, even though she felt sad inside. That's just how it is to love someone, she thought.

At night, she dreamed that Hoppsasa came hopping out of the forest because she missed Rakel. But after Rakel had grieved for the rabbit for three weeks, Mamma had brought her the poster. Rakel hung it on the wall above her desk. She thought it was the greatest comfort she could have wished for.

But this time, she has nobody to comfort her. This is something she can never tell anyone. Mamma would be so terribly ashamed if she found out what Rakel has done—and everyone would think that she's a bad mother. Mamma, who has sacrificed her entire life for Rakel. Who has moved to a country where everyone looks down on her.

Poor Mamma, who is always so afraid. Who hides in the bedroom whenever the doorbell rings. Who sleeps with an ax in the bed when Pappa is away. Who carried a knife in her handbag the only time she went to the cinema alone—she had been willing to risk her life to see the movie about Mahatma Gandhi. When she got home, she was so out of breath she couldn't speak.

It had almost all gone terribly wrong. As she came out of the cinema, a man had come straight toward her, and she had only just managed to run across to the taxi before he could assault her. That's what happens when Pappa and Rakel don't pay closer attention. It's down to nothing but sheer luck that Rakel still has a mamma.

THE THIRTEENTH OF December. St. Lucy's Day. Rakel and Jakob's day. Rakel is on her way home from a doctor's appointment. Like an extinguished St. Lucy, she walks across the snow-covered fields, the snow sighing mournfully beneath her boots. When she gets down to Kringstad road and looks back over the fields she's just crossed, her footsteps look like symbols on a white sheet of paper. As if she has written a Christmas letter to the sky. Will she ever receive a reply?

It starts to snow. Big, white flakes that flutter slowly down through the air. It's so quiet. She sticks out her tongue and catches a few of the snowflakes, letting them melt in her mouth, so she can experience the taste of the dying snow. Then she sees it. The snowflakes are the sky's Christmas letter to the earth. Yes—of course she received a reply.

Jakob sends her a Christmas gift, even though she's forbidden him from contacting her. It's a collection of short stories by Alice Munro, *Too Much Happiness*. The title story is about Sofia Kovalevskaya, who is unhappily in love and contracts pneumonia on her way home to Stockholm after having visited her beloved Maksim in Genoa, on the Italian Riviera. It's too much for her heart. And Sofia's last words here in the world are: "Too much happiness."

She reads *Tess of the D'Urbervilles* again. One of the five books Jakob has said he would choose to take with him to a desert island, should a journalist ever call up and ask him. As she reads, it occurs to her that Tess might be similar to the girls that take Jakob's fancy in reality:

She was a fine and handsome girl—not handsomer than some others, possibly—but her mobile peony mouth and large innocent eyes added eloquence to color and shape. . . . She was so modest, so expressive, she had looked so soft in her thin white gown that he felt he had acted stupidly.

She enjoys the descriptions of the landscapes, the way they are woven into the plot. But it is right at the very end of the book that the miracle happens, one of the universe's magical junctures. Because what does Tess say to her beloved when she wakes at Stonehenge on that final day and realizes that her life is over? "This happiness could not have lasted. It was too much." *Too much happiness.*

SPRING IS THE saddest of the seasons. May, with its bright green joie de vivre. The contrast between the life around her and the death inside her. She understands all too well why Heinrich Heine chose May:

Im wunderschönen Monat Mai,
als alle Knospen sprangen,
da ist in meinem Herzen
die Liebe aufgegangen.

Rakel lies in bed listening to *Dichterliebe* by Schumann, with tenor Fritz Wunderlich. From the concert he performed in Salzburg on her birthday, nine years before she was born. And she thinks that this might just be the most beautiful interpretation she's ever heard. The lyrical timbre of his voice—it makes her want to laugh and cry at the same time. Then she learns that he too died young, at just thirty-five years old.

She plays the songs over and over again. Finds comfort in being able to bury all her love and pain in a sunken chest at the bottom of the sea:

Wisst ihr, warum der Sarg wohl
so gross und schwer mag sein?
Ich senkt' auch meine Liebe
und meinen Schmerz hinein.

. . .

These are the last words he sings. But then it isn't the end after all, because the piano postlude simply carries on and on. Like a promise that life goes on. It's the most hopeful postlude she's ever heard.

The composer Robert Schumann also waited eight years for his beloved. Rakel is fascinated by Schumann's story—how he was miserably in love with the young pianist Clara Wieck when he was composing *Dichterliebe* to texts from *Das Buch der Lieder*. In these poems by Heinrich Heine, he finds sympathy for the love, uncertainty, and despair he feels.

Clara is only eight years old when he hears her play at a concert for the first time. Schumann himself is seventeen, and so captivated by her playing that he abandons studying law in order to take piano lessons from her father. He takes up lodgings in a room in the Wieck family home and becomes like a big brother to Clara. When Clara is thirteen, they develop deeper feelings for one another, and two years later they declare their love.

But Clara's father refuses to allow them to see each other and orders the letters they send one another to be burned. They meet in secret. Schumann might wait at a café for hours, just to be able to spend a few brief moments with Clara after she has performed one of her concerts. When Clara turns eighteen, Schumann asks her father for her hand in marriage. But Clara's father doesn't want his daughter to throw her life away on a poor composer. Schumann has to fight a long, hard battle before they are finally permitted to marry in 1840, on the day before Clara turns twenty-one. The same year that Schumann completes *Dichterliebe*.

It's as if she can hear his pain in the music. How the final unresolved piano chord in the opening song, "Im wunderschönen Monat Mai," expresses his unfulfilled longing. And how the uncertainty in his love is emphasized through the uncertainty in his choice of musical key:

when the piano strikes the first chords, it sounds as if the song is in F sharp minor, but when the singing voice begins the actual melody, it sounds like A major.

It's similar to what she fell for in the Violin Sonata by César Franck. How in the music the joy and sorrow are so tightly interwoven that it's impossible to tell them apart. César Franck is a master of key changes. He modulates his themes, weaving them into each other and inverting them, so that they continually appear in new ways, only with a slight twist. The entire sonata has a cyclical form, where the themes from one movement appear again in later movements, but often transformed. She hopes that one day she might manage to write a novel in the same way.

César Franck was a mature man when he composed the Violin Sonata in 1886. Almost thirty years older than Rakel is now.

THE MOST PAINFUL thing is not having anyone to talk to. The most painful thing is bearing the loss all alone. That she has promised never to speak of this.

No. Most painful of all is the shame. Not daring to tell anyone about it. Fearing that nobody will like her if they find out who she really is. What she had once been capable of doing.

Wonderful. The word she has always found far too big. Nora waited eight years too. Perhaps it wasn't her disappointment in Helmer that was the worst, but the transition from gold to granite. That what she thought was a noble act, a sacrifice made for love, became a sin. That she was not the savior, but the one who needed saving. And perhaps the wonderful state she longed for was to one day feel free of guilt. Without shame.

JAKOB IS STILL with her in everything she does. It seems impossible to find even the tiniest morsel of her life that has not been infiltrated by him. She misses him in a way that makes her see him everywhere—even though she's lying in bed.

When she reads the relationships column in *A-magasinet*, she's sure that it's Jakob who has written in to ask for advice under the heading "Lost Love." He still misses her, he writes, and wonders whether it really is possible to love someone for the rest of your life, and whether he will always regret the choice he's made. Everything fits. The voice. That they met when his youngest daughter was still a newborn. That it was as if he came alive when he met her. That at home his family just thinks he's a silent oddball. That he feels boundless admiration for her, but cannot fail his children.

There are just a couple of details that give her pause. Like the fact that he writes that he has a child he doesn't live with. But instead of wondering whether it really is Jakob who has written the letter, she gets angry at Jakob for having kept this child a secret. But this thing with the child might also be a red herring, something he's added in order to make sure that nobody else realizes he's the one who has written the letter. Nobody but her. Because he knows that she'll recognize his voice no matter what. And that she will understand that this is actually a kind of love letter he has written to her, because it's the only way he can reach her since she's forbidden him from contacting her directly.

She squirrels away the column with other things she has kept over the years: the ferry ticket from when she went home with him to peruse the contents of his bookshelves. The receipt from the hotel they stayed at in Copenhagen. And the thing she's most ashamed of: a used condom. Its contents have long since congealed and turned brown, but she can't bring herself to throw it away, because it might just contain enough biological matter to enable her to clone a copy of him at some point in the future.

SHE LIES IN bed and is hungry, but doesn't have the strength to go to the kitchen and prepare something to eat. Instead, she lies there wondering whether it would have been better to end up in prison. In prison, all her meals would be served to her, and she'd have an hour of social contact with the other inmates every day. Maybe visits from the prison priest too. The problem is finding a crime she has the conscience to commit, and strength enough to carry out.

She thinks of something Jakob once told her about Sophus Lie. In 1870, when he was in his late twenties, he set out from Paris to Milan on foot to visit a renowned professor of mathematics. But he didn't get very far. The Franco-Prussian War had just broken out, and a wandering foreigner naturally aroused suspicion. The French searched his knapsack and found papers filled with incomprehensible mathematical symbols that convinced them he must be a German spy. He therefore had to spend several months as a French prisoner of war, a time he used to write much of his doctoral thesis. "One of my best periods of work," he later said of his time in prison.

"Mathematicians are unusually well suited to life under lock and key," Jakob had concluded.

But what does a mathematician do when her head is full of syrup? A mathematician who can't think straight enough to do mathematics?

SHE FINDS A book in English, *Little Sparrow: A Portrait of Sophia Kova-levsky*, and begins to read about Sofia's life. Sofia, who writes poetry as a little girl, and is so fond of rhyme and rhythm. Who is shy, with dark, curly hair and soulful green eyes like canned gooseberries. Who has a lively face that is wide-awake one minute, deep in a daydream the next, and that exhibits a peculiar mix of childish naivete and great depth of thought. Sofia, who has such a hungry heart that it swells for anyone who gives her a few friendly words or seems especially fond of her, but who just as quickly shuts out those who disappoint her or favor others.

The way she still looks like a young girl long after becoming a woman, and is taken for being much younger than she is. Who is so physically slender and quick that she is given the nickname Little Sparrow. Her childishness and playfulness, which she retains to the end of her life. The fact that she doesn't pay much attention to her appearance and is slightly unkempt—and the positive first impression she makes on the people she meets nonetheless.

After having met her for the first time in 1876 when she was twenty-six years old, the Swedish mathematician Gösta Mittag-Leffler described Sofia in a letter to a friend:

> As a woman, she is splendid. She is beautiful, and when she
> speaks, her face is illuminated by an expression of feminine

kindness and superior intelligence that is almost blinding. Her manner is simple and natural, without the slightest trace of pedantry or pretention. In addition, she is in all respects "une dame du grand monde." As a scholar, she is characterized by her unusual clarity and precision of expression and by her quick powers of perception. Nor is it hard to see the in-depth nature of her studies, and I fully understand why Weierstrass would regard her as the most gifted of all his students.

Another of Sofia's long-term admirers, Sergey Lamansky, wrote after her death in 1891:

It is hard to reconcile oneself to such a loss. It would be difficult to find another woman who exhibits such a happy blend of intellect, talent, gaiety, and vivacity.

Sofia's cousin, Sophie von Adelung, wrote in an article that Sofia had an unbelievably versatile nature and threw herself into everything that appealed to her imagination, emotions, and intellect. She developed these three aspects of her personality with great enthusiasm and passion.

Rakel notes the less attractive traits too. Like the fact that Sofia expects too much from friendship. That she overlooks everything else—including those closest to her—during the periods in which she is entirely engrossed in her work. That she doesn't appreciate the value of practical housework, and does everything in as slapdash a manner as possible. In a letter, Sofia writes:

All these stupid, practical things that cannot be postponed are a test of my patience, and I am starting to understand why men so appreciate good, practical housewives. Were I a man, I would choose for myself a beautiful little wife who could liberate me from all this.

WHEN RAKEL WAS small, Mamma taught her how to catch flies in a jam jar and let them out of the house without harming them. So that Rakel wouldn't risk becoming a fly herself in the next life. Even though Rakel isn't a Buddhist, she still carries flies and spiders out into freedom. What if the people who believe in reincarnation are right? What if everyone is continually reborn as new versions of themselves, only with a slight twist? Then maybe it might be possible to recognize the former lives you once lived, the people you have been.

If those who believe in reincarnation are right, Rakel might have been Sofia Kovalevskaya in a past life. Sofia was also discovered by a much older professor who took care of her. But Sofia was a friend of the author Fyodor Dostoevsky, and in that regard Rakel has little to offer for the moment, although she thinks she could have become friends with the Author.

And then there's the mystery—the fact that Sofia abandoned mathematics and began to write literature. Rakel has also abandoned mathematics, in a way. And although she hasn't written any literature just yet, she has the sense that she's about to do so.

Perhaps she will never get to know the Author in reality, but she's found a nugget of gold in one of his novels. The kind of space that expands her, opening a new world of wondrous possibilities. The space between F sharp and G flat. She's always thought of F sharp and G flat as the same note—the black key between F and G on the piano. But the Author has written about the space between F sharp and G flat as a space that only the truly great violinists are familiar with, one that separates the superstars from the mediocre. This is the space to which she must find the key. Then she will be able to write.

THE WORST THING about time is that it stands still. When she doesn't have the strength to fill it.

No. The worst thing about time is that it passes. The way everything ends up being too late. There should be a deduction for the time in which you can hardly be said to be living.

AN ARITHMETIC PROBLEM:

Age at which illness first appeared: 25 years

Current age: 35 years

Average residual capacity during period of illness: 20 percent, or $^1/_5$

Adjustment factor during period of illness: 1 illness-adjusted year = 5 calendar years

New estimated illness-adjusted age: $25 + (35-25)/5 = 27$ years

In which case she still has $5 \times (30-27) = 15$ calendar years left before she effectively turns 30.

But it probably won't help to submit this calculation to the Literary Council of the Norwegian Authors' Union. She will never have the chance to win the Tarjei Vesaas' Debutant Prize, awarded to a debut author aged thirty or under.

It's no use presenting this calculation to her ovaries either. They tirelessly forge ahead at a speed of one follicle per month. When the store is empty, it will be too late.

RAKEL LIES IN bed, wondering what Jakob would say if he was with her right now. Something funny, perhaps. She always had to laugh when she was with him, although she often didn't even understand why.

Like the time they were at a conference and a famous mathematician spent half his presentation standing facing the blackboard, scratching his head. Rakel had been irritated by the fact that he apparently didn't value his audience's time enough to go to the trouble of preparing properly. Still, the audience sat there reverently, looking at him. Jakob leaned toward her and whispered, almost as in the nursery rhyme:

> A-tisket, a-tasket,
> a Sierpinski gasket.
> He had a thought about a proof,
> But on the way he lost it.
> He lost it, he lost it,
> And on the way he lost it.
> A little boy has picked it up
> and put it in his pocket.

She'd had to fold herself over the desk so that nobody would see how hard she was laughing.

Jakob. Who could tickle her soul in just the way it needed to be tickled. Who mirrored her, so that she caught a glimpse of herself from the outside, as he saw her. Who else can reflect her now? When she was little, she had David. Even though he was just an imaginary friend. Now she has no one. Nobody she can lean her loneliness against.

She takes out the book about Sofia Kovalevskaya, *Little Sparrow*. If those who believe in reincarnation are right, perhaps it might help to study Sofia's life, so she can avoid repeating the same mistakes. If you don't have friends among the living, you must seek company among the dead.

SOUNDS AND LIGHT make her brain run wild, but too much silence can make her crazy too. She turns on the radio. NRK Alltid Klassisk is playing Mozart's great G Minor Symphony. The first time she heard it was in the car with Mamma and Pappa. They're in Germany, and there's a long line for the ferry across to Denmark. Pappa has purchased a new cassette player, and Rakel is allowed to choose which cassette she wants to listen to. She selects the one with a rainbow of colors on the front.

And then Mozart enters her life. He fills the entire car with the first movement from Symphony No. 40, as the voices of Mamma and Pappa hum away up front. When she stretches out, making herself as long as possible across the back seat, she can touch one of the car doors with her fingertips and the other with her toes. It feels as if the entire world is encapsulated within the car. Nice and safe. She wants the line for the ferry never to end; she wants to stay in the car forever. Pappa, Mamma, Mozart, and her. Together on summer vacation.

"Pappa, I have to pee," says Mamma.

"They probably have a restroom in the waiting area over there by the ferry landing," Pappa says.

"I daren't go over there alone," Mamma says.

"But Suriwan, honey," Pappa says. "I can't get out of the car when we're in the line waiting to drive aboard."

"How do you say *toilet* in German?" asks Mamma.

"Toiletten," replies Pappa. "But I'm sure they'll understand you if you ask in English too."

"But what if I can't find my way back?" says Mamma.

"We'll be in exactly the same place," says Pappa. "In the worst case, we'll just have moved a few spaces ahead."

"I'll never find you again," says Mamma.

"But Suriwan, honey," replies Pappa. "It's right over there."

"I almost can't hold it," says Mamma. "There's a good chance I might pee myself right here in the car."

Rakel can see that Pappa thinks Mamma should pull herself together. But Mamma is so afraid—Rakel has to help her.

"Mamma, Mamma, I know what you can do. You can count how many cars there are in front of us in the line, and then you can count the same number of cars when you come back. And if you don't find us then, Mamma, you just have to walk forward. Because we'll definitely be up that way. You won't need to look back, Mamma. Just walk up and up until you find us again. And if you don't find us in the line, you just have to get on the ferry, Mamma. Because if you can't find us, we'll already be on board. And if you don't find us on the ferry, you don't need to be afraid, Mamma. Because then *we'll* find *you*."

"Rakel is the only one who understands me," Mamma says. "She understands me always."

"Maybe Rakel can go to the restroom with you," says Pappa. "Perhaps you'll dare go to the restroom if you're escorted by a four-year-old?"

WHEN RAKEL IS ill, it's Mamma who prepares food for her. She makes dinner from scratch. Rakel has become allergic to additives, and Mamma chops vegetables for hours so that Rakel's body will be able to absorb the nutrients. Pappa goes out to buy groceries so that she doesn't have to go to the store. She doesn't have the strength to do all this herself. Thanks to Mamma and Pappa, she can spend her life doing more than just surviving—it's because of them that she has the energy to read a little each day. On good days, she's even able to write a little. What would she do without them?

"Would you like meat or fish for dinner?" asks Mamma.

"Just whatever is easiest," says Rakel.

"I'll give you the best cut of meat," says Mamma.

"Why don't you take the best one?" asks Rakel. "I can't see any difference between them anyway."

"I always give the best to you," says Mamma. "Today I ate the old slices from yesterday's bread, so that you could have the fresh loaf."

"But I don't have anything against eating yesterday's bread," says Rakel. "Next time, take whichever bread you think is best for yourself."

"It's only because of me that you had a banana for breakfast this morning," says Mamma. "I was going to eat it, but when I saw that it was the last one, I saved it for you, even though I didn't have anything else to put on my bread."

Rakel sighs. "I could have just taken an apple instead. You should stop making so many sacrifices, Mamma."

"I sacrifice everything for you," Mamma says. "And I have done ever since you were born. Who's going to do all this for me when I get old?"

WHEN SOFIA'S MOTHER saw her newborn daughter for the first time, she was so disappointed that she cried and turned away. She already had a daughter, six-year-old Anyuta, who was blond and beautiful and the spitting image of her mother. Both parents adored her. But this newborn baby had none of her mother's refined features; she was more like her father.

For six years, they had hoped for a son, who might one day be able to take over the family estate. An heir. They didn't need another daughter, and so Sofia's mother left her in the care of the nursemaid. Five years later came the longed-for son, Fyodor, who received even more attention from his parents than Anyuta had.

When the family had guests, Sofia's mother told the nursemaid to dress Anyuta and Fyodor in their finest clothes and present them to their visitors. The nursemaid related that she had also dressed Sofia in her finery and asked that she be allowed to join in. But Sofia was shy, and turned away when the guests spoke to her. She fell silent, and refused to answer their questions. In the end, her mother ended up blurting out: "Well, nursemaid, you may take the little beast away. She does nothing but embarrass us in front of our guests!"

There was an age difference of twenty-one years between Sofia's parents. In her memoirs, Sofia writes that her father treated her mother more like a daughter than a wife. When he married her, he was forty-four years old; she was young and beautiful, with a quick mind and a rare gift for spreading joy to those around her. He had appreciated this last trait in particular.

Sofia's mother also had a better education than most girls at the time. She spoke four languages fluently, was widely read in classic and modern literature, and was musically gifted. But she had never learned the practical side of running a household, and the estate's servants did not intend to submit to an inexperienced newcomer. So she became like a guest in her own house, while Sofia's father let the servants manage the household just as it had always been managed.

Despite having married, Sofia's father didn't wish to let go of his former bachelor life entirely. He still participated in the pleasures of the night with old friends. They gambled and went to nightclubs, where they were entertained by gypsies. In her diary, Sofia's mother confesses that she feels lonely. "The devil's jealousy torments me," she writes, after learning that one of the women who entertained at the club was possibly her husband's former mistress. "Our anniversary. My husband is at the club, where the gypsies sing," her diary states.

What did Sofia do when her mother was unhappy? Did she spy on her through the cracked door? Long to creep up into her lap? Braid her long hair, stroke her cheek? She probably knew that she wouldn't be able to manage it, that she would only stain the dress her mother was wearing or tangle her hair. Thank goodness her mother had Anyuta and Fyodor to comfort her, or she may never have survived otherwise.

But at least Sofia was spared having to be an only child. Spared carrying the responsibility alone.

Rakel glimpses a little girl standing behind the door, a little girl who doesn't know how to make her mother happy. She's afraid to disturb her, and yet afraid she'll regret it if she doesn't at least try. She's always afraid of regretting not having tried. Perhaps she's thinking of something her mother has said: "I wish I had been more grateful toward my own mother, appreciated her more while she was alive. She died when I was young, and now it's too late. Now I have to regret this for the rest of my life, thinking of everything she did for me. I hope you'll be spared all this regret when I die."

The girl has already done so much she can regret. Not paid attention when dinner was ready, wanting to finish her drawing first or the chapter of the book she was reading. She's an ungrateful child. But on the other hand, she's always afraid that somebody will die, and that she will have done something she'll then have to regret for the rest of her life.

Perhaps the mother catches sight of the girl behind the crack in the door and beckons her over. Talks about why she's so unhappy, all she has sacrificed. Because the girl is the only one who understands. The only one who can comfort her. *If you ever have to choose between a man who loves you and a man you love, choose the one who loves you. That's the mistake people make in life.*

RAKEL GOOGLES "HUMAN metrics" and brings up the personality test she took ages ago. Perhaps she might get a different result this time? Maybe she's changed? But she gets the same letters as before, INFJ, only with slightly different numerical values. Apparently she can never escape herself.

But when she reads the description of this personality type, she discovers something Jakob didn't read aloud to her. "The most fearful of all personality types," it says. "They often struggle with internal conflicts and are the personality type that most often needs to seek help from a psychologist." There's also a list of famous people with this personality type: Leo Tolstoy, Fyodor Dostoevsky, Mahatma Gandhi, Mother Teresa. And Jesus. But also Adolf Hitler.

Perhaps it isn't so strange that Jesus turned out the way he did, regardless of whether God exists. Imagine having a mother who says you are the Son of God, that she was impregnated by the Holy Spirit. And if what she claimed wasn't true, she must have felt so ashamed at his conception that she made the story up. As a child, you do your best to live up to the story—even if it means sacrificing yourself on the cross. You do anything to help your mother. Poor Jesus.

Maybe she can write her difficult second novel before she's even begun her first? She already has the opening:

Mamma says that I'm the Son of God. The one everyone's been waiting for, who will save the world. When I was small, all the boys my age were killed because of me. I don't understand how the world could have been waiting for something like that. Or how I'm ever going to be able to make up for it.

IF MAMMA HADN'T had Rakel, she would have been able to move back to her country and remain a teacher at the university. Instead of having to sacrifice so much for Rakel's sake. Rakel has seen just how Mamma can be when she's happy. Like the summer they went on vacation to see Grandpa, and Mamma was suddenly someone who could do anything—the person everyone admired. The university lecturer whose old students stopped by to say hello. The center of a friendship group. The prettiest and funniest of them all.

Poor Mamma, who has a recurring dream that she is lost. "Isn't it strange that I constantly dream the same thing?" Mamma says. "We're hiking in the forest, but then I get lost. You and Pappa just keep going, even though I'm calling your names. I'm so afraid that you won't come back and save me."

"It's just a bad dream, Mamma," says Rakel. "I would never leave you like that in real life."

"You've always loved Pappa more than you love me," says Mamma. "Even if I was willing to sacrifice everything for you."

Rakel sighs. "I know how much you have sacrificed," she says.

"But you don't know how difficult it has been," says Mamma. "When you were little, it was almost impossible for me to talk to people when you were around. You got so embarrassed when my Norwegian wasn't perfect. I almost felt as if I couldn't say anything at all."

Rakel remembers how embarrassing she thought it was, but it wasn't because Mamma spoke broken Norwegian. It was because she didn't understand what people asked her, and so answered inappropriately. Then the person Mamma was talking to would look at Rakel with a curious expression, as if they wondered whether she understood what Mamma meant. But Rakel couldn't explain that Mamma had misunderstood when Mamma herself was pretending to understand.

She thinks of the time she and Mamma took the bus into the city alone. Mamma gave Rakel three kroner to pay for the tickets. But the bus driver said that it wasn't enough. From the start of the year, the price had increased by one kroner.

"She child," said Mamma.

"Yep, no doubt about it." The bus driver smiled. "But it's still four kroner."

"She five," Mamma said.

"Yep, and a very cute five-year-old she is too," answered the bus driver.

"Five øre?" asked Mamma, rummaging around in her purse to pull out a five-øre coin, which she gave to the driver. Then she went and sat down.

Rakel stood there, wondering what she should do. She had only fifty øre in her pocket, which Mamma had given her to buy marbles. It wasn't enough. Perhaps she could ask the driver if she could ride the bus halfway into the city, then get off and walk the rest of the way. But what if she got lost? And how would she find Mamma again?

"No, you keep your fifty øre and go take a seat." The kind bus driver smiled.

IT'S AS IF her body no longer knows the difference between night and day. After all, it only lies there in bed regardless. She turns on the bedside lamp and flicks through the pages of the album of newspaper clippings that Mamma has kept. If there is a Creator, making childhood come first was one of his better ideas, because then you have something to sustain you for the rest of your life.

On the first page, Mamma has glued in the certificate Rakel received when she won her first drawing competition. Rakel is five years old. It's a Saturday, and she's sitting at the kitchen table. The radio is on, a program called Music Kindergarten. Then something hits her in the diaphragm. It's a piece of music. She didn't catch what the piece was called or who the composer is. She simply sits there, listening to the music and marveling at all the beautiful images it creates within her. Afterward, she learns that it's the *Nutcracker Suite* by Tchaikovsky, "Dance of the Reed Pipes."

She hears the story of little Clara, who is given a nutcracker doll as a gift by the mysterious Herr Drosselmeyer. Rakel draws a large nutcracker doll dancing pirouettes in the center of the page. A little girl stands there, watching him. She holds three golden nuts in her hand. Three ballerinas are dancing on the tips of their toes, trying to avoid all the mice scurrying across the floor. A man wearing a black cape and top hat plays the piano in the background. And all the toys have come alive, and are dancing in a ring around the Christmas tree.

The next Saturday, the presenters on the radio talk about her drawing. She wins a book as her prize: *Ferdinand the Flute Player*. The book is still on the shelf above the desk.

She turns the pages of the album and finds a review of the concert at which she was a soloist with an orchestra for the first time. Just before she was about to go on stage, Rakel had been nervous. She had a stomachache. But when she begins to play, she enjoys disappearing into the music completely. She mustn't think, because that's when things can go wrong. She just has to *feel*. To trust that her fingers know where they are going, that her ring finger won't miss the F sharp when shifting to third position on the A string. After all, it never usually misses that leap.

Afterward, several people from the audience came up to her, asking how her fingers could move so quickly and nimbly, how she managed to create such a fine spiccato with her bow. But most of all, Rakel remembers the old woman with tears in her eyes who hugged her.

At the very back of the album she discovers the poem that was published in the newspaper when she was sixteen years old, "Autumn Dance." In the very same newspaper that Bjørnstjerne Bjørnson had once been able to see his first article in print, "Frihedens tale til Moldenserne." And Bjørnson ended up being awarded the Nobel Prize in literature, even though it was really Ibsen who deserved it. The poem is high-flown and exudes a youthful grandiloquence, but she recognizes something in it all the same. The timbre of autumn.

AS A CHILD, Sofia seemed cheerful and spirited. She was skeptical of strangers, but when she was with people she liked, she could talk the hind legs off a donkey. The words tumbled out of her, helter-skelter, especially when she became excited. Her tutor, Josef Malevich, described his young pupil as a wide-eyed child with an insatiable appetite for all he could teach her. But he had greater hopes for her literary talents than her mathematical ones:

> One day, I sat for a long time thinking of the unusual achievements of my talented pupil and her possible future. What if fate were to permit her a higher education, which is unfortunately inaccessible to women at our universities? What if the same fate were to deprive her of all financial means, forcing her to have to write in order to survive? Then I am sure my talented student would attain a high position in the literary world.

But it was mathematics that Sofia ended up studying. Since the universities in her homeland were closed to women, she traveled to Heidelberg, where she convinced the professors to allow her to attend the lectures. Her friend Julia Lermontova, who shared an apartment with Sofia during that first year of study, describes a happy time at the university in Heidelberg:

After having begun her studies, Sofia was filled with an ardent enthusiasm. But her serious search for knowledge in no way prevented her from finding joy in even the smallest, seemingly trivial things. When we were together, Sofia and I might suddenly begin to race down the road like two small children. My God, so much joy there is in these memories from our early days at the university. Sofia's outstanding abilities, her love of mathematics, and her unusually sympathetic personality attracted everyone she met. There was something absolutely adorable about her. All her professors were thrilled at her talents; she was also hardworking and could sit at her desk for hours, immersed in mathematical calculations. Her high moralistic ideals were accompanied by a deep and complex spiritual psyche, the like of which I have never encountered again.

Sofia's professors described her as "something completely out of the ordinary," and news of the curious Russian girl spread all across the little town. People even began to turn their heads to look at her on the street. But Sofia retained her quiet ways. In her interactions with professors and other students, she was always extremely shy and anxious; she spoke only to her fellow students when absolutely necessary in connection with her studies. Still, rumors of her exceptional ability circulated throughout the student body; one described how, during a lecture, she had blushingly approached the blackboard to show the professor a mistake he hadn't been able to find himself.

Women were not permitted to sit for exams at the university, so the only option Sofia had for further study was to find a private tutor. She decided to travel to Berlin to seek out Karl Weierstrass, Europe's most influential mathematician.

The years Sofia spent studying in Berlin were lonely ones, and she became more and more of a recluse. Her meetings with Weierstrass were the only social contact she had, other than the time she spent with her friend Julia. According to Julia, Sofia had a tendency to lose herself completely in mathematics:

Her ability to devote herself to focused mental work for many hours at a stretch, without leaving her desk, was truly astonishing. And when, after having spent all day engrossed in heavy thought, she at long last pushed her papers aside and got up from her chair, she was always so consumed by her thoughts that she began to wander back and forth about the room, taking quick steps, which would eventually transition into a run, as she spoke aloud to herself and occasionally erupted into laughter. At such times, she seemed completely detached from reality, carried away by an imagination that led her beyond the boundaries of the present. . . .

She was never at peace, always setting new goals for herself, always passionately longing to achieve them. Despite this, I never saw her so despondent as when she had achieved a particular goal. It seemed the reality of her achievement never corresponded to what she had imagined. . . . Her ever-shifting moods, from sorrow to joy, made her an extremely interesting person to know.

Weierstrass opened his home to Sofia, inviting her to celebrate Christmas with him and his family when she didn't make the journey home to her family in Russia. He treated her as an equal and introduced her to the theory of Abelian functions. He claimed that it took him longer to solve mathematical problems when she wasn't around; she had an ability to make intuitive associations, the like of which he had never seen even among the great mathematicians. He worried about her constantly and urged her to take breaks from her studies, to get some fresh air and look after her health.

"There is much in this friendship that is poetic, ideal, and openhearted, and it gives me an enormous amount of happiness and delight," Sofia wrote in a letter. But at the same time, she denied the rumors that she was in a romantic relationship with Weierstrass.

JAKOB BELIEVED THAT the age difference of thirty-five years was too great for Sofia to have been interested in Weierstrass. But even as a child, Sofia had been infatuated with a much older man, her uncle Fyodor. Who not only lit the first intellectual sparks within her, but also was a source of intense pangs of jealousy. Every afternoon, he would lift her onto his lap and tell her about scientific discoveries. This was the highlight of five-year-old Sofia's daily routine.

But one day, another little girl around the same age as Sofia came to visit. Sofia was afraid the girl would disrupt the conversation with her uncle. So she made the girl promise she would keep her distance, and in return Sofia would let her choose all the games they would play that day. But when Sofia's uncle came to collect her in the afternoon, the treacherous girl asked if she could join them, despite the promise she had made.

"Of course," Sofia's uncle answered in a friendly voice.

"But she won't understand any of the things we talk about," Sofia protested.

"Well then, we'll have to talk about something she *can* understand," her uncle answered.

Sofia was furious at the girl for not keeping her side of the bargain, even after Sofia had spent all day playing the stupid games the girl had dictated. So when Sofia's uncle tried to lift Sofia up onto his lap, she resisted and took herself off into a corner to sulk. Her uncle looked at her in surprise.

Then he turned to the other girl and said, "Well, if Sofia doesn't want to sit on my lap, perhaps you would like to do so instead?"

The girl didn't need to be asked twice. She clambered up, taking Sofia's place. Sofia stood there, staring at the girl, who was radiant with happiness there in Sofia's uncle's lap. Before she even knew what she was doing, Sofia had rushed forward and bitten the girl on the arm, so hard that blood ran from the wound.

Rakel imagines how Sofia fought to resist Weierstrass's advances for an entire year. The butterflies in her stomach when he looked at her. Those St. Bernard eyes that drew her in, photographing her on their retinas. But then one day, in his study: the first kiss. The loosening of her bonnet. Locks of her hair falling around them like a tent. His hands on her hips. His lips at the base of her throat, then around her nipples. The voice that whispers in her ear, "It can hurt a little the first time. After that, it gets better." The stab of pain as he enters her. And afterward, the warmth. The warmth that from here on after, she will be unable to live without.

PAPPA WANTS RAKEL to take a walk to Kringstadsetra with him. "You're wasting away before our very eyes," he says. "I can pull you up the steepest hills, just as we used to do."

Most of the time she doesn't even have the strength to walk to the mailbox at the end of the drive. And even on days when she feels a little better, she still doesn't dare leave the house. What if she bumps into the woman from the Labor and Welfare Administration, who said that Rakel had to join the "Active Days" exercise scheme? There are ball games on Mondays, a mountain hike on Tuesdays, swimming on Wednesdays, jogging on Thursdays, and a get-together at a café on Fridays.

Had she the strength to do all this, she would have much rather been at work. So she wouldn't have to be a burden on society. So she'd be spared having to feel so useless.

She can't bear the curious gazes of the neighbors either. "If you can manage to go out for a walk, perhaps you should try going to work instead?" they say. They don't see how she has to lie in bed for days, gathering her strength to leave the house, and then ends up bedridden afterward. She's so tired of having to defend herself.

"Oh, how are you doing? You certainly *look* well, anyway. Everyone feels worn out from time to time, but you just have to pull yourself together and get to work. It's far too easy to abuse the welfare system these days."

But she gets that it's hard for others to understand. Had she not experienced this illness herself, she probably wouldn't have understood it either. Although she hopes she wouldn't have assumed that someone would choose to spend their life in bed out of pure laziness.

The incessant headache. The exhaustion after insignificant exertion. The erratic fever. Always feeling as if she's been knocked out by the flu or has run a marathon all night. Having a body that never quite manages to restore itself. She can force it to complete the activity there and then, but is always punished for it afterward. A delayed reaction, which makes it hard to restrain herself in time. She's so tired of never being able to do the things she wants to. Of looking forward to activities she doesn't manage to go through with after all.

Average capacity per day: 90 minutes (maximum 15 minutes continuous activity)

Breakfast: 10 minutes

Lunch: 15 minutes

Dinner: 20 minutes (including rest break)

Dressing and undressing: 5 minutes

Showering, brushing of teeth, and use of toilet: 30 minutes

Total time taken for meals and personal hygiene: 80 minutes

Available time for other activities (completion of Labor and Welfare Administration activity form, payment of bills, etc.): 10 minutes

Note: If the patient is served breakfast, lunch, and dinner in bed, this frees 45 minutes for other activities.

Other account terms: Any accrued remaining balance may be transferred to the next day, but the maximum accrued balance shall never exceed 120 minutes. The patient is therefore able to gather strength for greater indulgences, such as doctors' appointments and meetings with the Labor and Welfare Administration. Or possibly walks to Kringstadsetra.

Warning: In the event that the account becomes overdrawn, an overdraft fee of two bedridden weeks per hour will be charged.

RAKEL TRAILS HER fingers across the yellow patterned wallpaper above the bed, as if it is possible to seek comfort from the flowers there. She turns on the CD player that stands on the bedside table. "Besøk" by Jens Bjørneboe. Perhaps the most hopeful lyrics she's ever heard. She plays the song over and over again. It gives her peace, to feel that death is a friend.

She stares at the naked walls. Some paintings ought to be hanging there. She's allocated the spaces for them. But paintings are like men. It's rare that she finds one she could imagine having in the living room. And the few times this has happened, it's been too late—the painting was already sold. Even the time she arrived at the exhibition as soon as it opened, she hesitated too long. Someone else managed to buy the only painting she wanted. Above the bed, she could have had a painting like the one she saw in the pharmacy in Portugal. If only she'd had the courage to find out who the artist was.

Jakob once said that she needs to do better at getting out on the days she has the strength for it. "How do you think people are going to know that you exist if all you do is hide yourself away in bed?" he asked. "You should go to concerts, the theater, art galleries. Places where you have a chance to meet people like you."

It seems he was partly right. Going to art exhibitions won't find her any new friends, but she might just find a painting to keep her company.

SHE NOTICES THE painting straightaway. It's far too blue. She really needs warmer colors on the walls. Still she just can't bring herself to leave it—misses it as soon as she's back out on the street. It has a timbre to it that makes something vibrate within her. The golden tones in all that blue. The balance between the erased and the visible, the abstract and the concrete. The contrast between the movement of the hands and the concentrated peace of the face. She turns and walks back into the gallery.

It's a female violinist. Although she doesn't know how she can be sure of this, as the violin is part of what's been erased. A faint line hints at the violin's neck, as if the rest of the instrument has melted into the human body. Only the sensitivity of the fingers has been captured, along with the melancholy of the music.

But it's only when she gets home and turns the painting ninety degrees that the miracle reveals itself: the violinist is lying with her eyes closed. Her right hand is transformed into a face bending over her, the specter of a man. His black eye observes her with a combination of horror and tenderness, because the neck of the violin has become a sword that testifies to what has just happened. The violinist's left hand presses the sword against her throat. But the hand is no longer hers alone, it could just as easily be his.

Rakel turns the painting the right way up again, and the violinist rises, playing once more. But Rakel can now see the specter of threat in the background. The gold that ruptures. For the first time in her life she wishes she could paint, that she had painted this piece herself. She would have titled it "Play for Life / The Last Tenderness."

SHE GOES TO concerts too, when she has the strength for it. In order to have the feeling of still being a part of this world. To belong among people. To not always feel like a burden, or that she's in someone's way. She just wants to be someone who can sit on a front-row seat without thinking about it, without feeling inconsiderate; someone who calmly stays seated, even though the woman behind her whispers in annoyance to her husband that now she can't see anything; someone who doesn't have to assess whether she should turn around and apologize for sitting there—say that she understands how irritating it must be for those who were here first, and who possibly stood in line longer in order to ensure they would get the best seats, and who never thought anyone would be so inconsiderate as to sit in front of them; someone who doesn't have to consider whether she ought to move to the next vacant seat along; how she'll then block the view for someone else instead— and how fair is that just because they haven't complained yet?— because farther along all the seats are taken, and moving all the way to the back of the auditorium also feels unfair: Why shouldn't she be able to sit here just like anyone else—maybe even a taller person—would have sat here, had she not done so?

WHAT IS IT other women have that she lacks? Why would Jakob rather have Lea? Because Lea has given him children? Because she's magnanimous? Because Rakel is so ill? But he didn't want Rakel even when she was healthy; he only wanted her body. She had a talent for orgasms that surprised him. Just a couple of strokes with his hips, and she would be whisked away once more.

"It's never been better to be a man," he whispered. "I've never felt that I have so much to give another person. You're so wholehearted, present with your entire being."

And yet he still chose Lea.

Of moonlight nothing grows. Plants need sunlight to grow. But they can grow in artificial sunlight too. Indoors. Is there an artificial moonlight?

Correction: Of *real* moonlight nothing grows. But of imagined moonlight, one can build the most beautiful castle in the air. Plants need sunlight to survive. But strawberry rhubarb grows most quickly in utter darkness. It reaches for the light. If only it grows tall enough, surely it will find the light it seeks? After a few weeks it gives up. Its life is shorter than that of its relatives. But it tastes sweeter. And has a warmer glow.

OF EVERYONE SOFIA knew, it was her older sister, Anyuta, who was closest to her. Sofia loved her and hated her at the same time. Her beautiful, blond sister, who could dominate a ball with her beauty from the time she was just eight years old. Whose shadow Sofia always walked in. Their father had once joked, "Our Anyuta can be sent straight to court when she grows up. She'd drive any czar crazy with the desire to do her bidding." Both sisters had taken this statement entirely at face value.

Anyuta—with a literary talent that made Fyodor Dostoevsky publish her first short stories in the literary magazine *Epoch*. In his first letter to her, Dostoevsky writes:

> *Your letter full of such kind and sincere confidence in me interested me so much that I immediately began reading the story you sent me. I must confess that I began reading not without a secret fear, for to editors of journals often falls the sad duty of disillusioning beginning writers who send us their first literary efforts for evaluation. But as I read, my fear was dissipated, and I more and more came under the enchantment of that youthful immediacy, that sincerity and warmth of feeling, with which your story is permeated. . . . I shall be happy sincerely if you find an opportunity to write me more about yourself; tell me your age*

and what are the circumstances of your life. Knowing this is
important for a correct evaluation of your talent.

Devoted to you,
F. D.

Dostoevsky continues to correspond with Anyuta, and invites both sisters to meet with him when they spend six weeks in St. Petersburg in the winter of 1865. Anyuta captivates Dostoevsky so intensely at their first encounter that he proposes to her just a short time later. He receives a provisional acceptance, on the condition that the engagement be kept secret. Not even Sofia may learn of it.

In order to hide his feelings for Anyuta, Dostoevsky turns more of his attention to Sofia. On several occasions, he gives her the impression that he favors her over her sister. He says that she has gypsy eyes and that she will be a great beauty when she comes of age. He praises the poems she has written, and says that her piano playing is the most talented and sensitive he has ever heard. Sofia eagerly soaks up these compliments. In her diary, she writes: "Dear God, let everyone in the world adore Anyuta and prefer her, but let me be beautiful in Fyodor Dostoevsky's eyes."

When she finally finds out that Dostoevsky has proposed to her sister, Sofia is crushed. But Anyuta ends up turning Dostoevsky down, explaining her decision to Sofia as follows: "He doesn't need a wife like me. His wife should devote herself entirely to him, give up her whole life for his sake and think only of him. This is something I cannot do. I want a life of my own."

Fifteen-year-old Sofia writes in her diary: "He proposed to the wrong sister!"

POOR SOFIA. WHAT did you do when you discovered that Dostoevsky actually wanted Anyuta? Did you sit at the piano and play Beethoven's

Sonata Pathétique, which you had so diligently practiced in order to impress him?

As you lift your gaze to receive your applause, you realize that the room is empty. Dostoevsky and Anyuta must have snuck out as you played. You go to look for them and find them in a dark nook deep in the library, sitting close to one another on the divan. Dostoevsky pale with emotion. With Anyuta's hands in his. Perhaps you also catch the words he whispers: "My beloved Anyuta, do you understand? I have loved you since the first moment I saw you, and before that I had intimations from your letters. The love I feel for you is not that of friendship, but of passion—the passion of my entire body."

In that moment, the whole world shatters for you. The dream of ever being loved.

Because if Dostoevsky, the man you love with all of your heart, cannot love you, then surely no one can.

1. According to the Bible, Jakob loved Rakel, not Lea.

2. It's the *R* and the *k* that are the problem. If only she could
   have gotten rid of them and read her name backward, then
   Jakob could have been hers.

"PAPPA, HAVE YOU been sent the invoice for our part of the new communal mailbox stand yet?" asks Mamma.

"Mm-hmm," says Pappa, trying to watch the evening news.

"Well, how much was it?"

"A thousand," says Pappa.

"*A thousand kroner?* Did they only give you the total amount, or was the invoice itemized?"

"It was itemized."

"Did they charge you for the work too, or just for the materials?"

Pappa turns up the volume on the TV in order to hear it better.

"Did the neighbors who put up the stand get out of having to pay for it?" Mamma asks.

Pappa shakes his head.

"Then did they pay the same as us?"

"I think they paid three hundred fifty," Pappa mumbles.

Mamma didn't hear what Pappa said, so she asks again. An irritated expression crosses Pappa's face. Rakel forgets that she's told herself not to get involved.

"He said they paid three fifty. And really, they shouldn't have paid anything seeing as they did all the work. A thousand kroner isn't that much."

"Do the two of you think I don't want to pay?" says Mamma. "I would have paid *two thousand* without saying anything."

Can't you please just shut up, thinks Rakel. It isn't even you who pays the bills. But Mamma won't let it go.

"Did you get a paper copy of the invoice, or did they send it by email?"

Pappa presses his headphones against his ears.

Mamma asks again.

"Does it matter?" asks Pappa.

"You always have to have secrets!" says Mamma.

"By email," Pappa says. He turns back to the TV screen, annoyed.

"Goodness, you can't even ask a question in this family!" Mamma exclaims.

Rakel gets up a little too abruptly, picking up her plate so she can take it with her to the kitchen and finish eating there.

"What's gotten into *you*?" shrieks Mamma. "I haven't even said anything!"

"I can't take any more of this!" Rakel hears someone shout. The voice is like her own, but it's in an unfamiliar key.

"We're not even arguing!" shouts Mamma.

"No, but I'm sitting here dreading it, just waiting for it to happen!" Rakel's new voice shouts back.

Mamma is breathing heavily; her entire body is shaking. But Rakel doesn't have the energy to comfort her now. She goes out to the kitchen, but feels Mamma's steps in her diaphragm. How Mamma goes into the bathroom to cry because no one understands her, and if not even Rakel loves her, then she may as well just die.

But Rakel forces herself to take a bite of her bread and chews slowly, the sticky mass expanding in her mouth until it becomes impossible to swallow. She imagines Mamma lying in the bathtub, wondering whether Rakel will find her before it's too late.

She tries the bathroom door. It isn't locked. Mamma is sitting on the lid of the toilet, in tears.

"I'm sorry, Mamma. I didn't mean to overreact like that. I don't know what came over me. It was as if I just lost control."

"I didn't even say anything," says Mamma.

"No, Mamma, you didn't do anything wrong."

"It makes me so upset when you do things like that," says Mamma. "You make me feel like a bad mamma."

"I'm sorry, Mamma. I shouldn't have reacted that way. You're the best mamma in all the world, and I don't know what I would do without you."

RAKEL IMAGINES SOFIA lying in bed, longing for a better life. A life in which she doesn't always have to play the role of comforter. She, Sofia, who is unable even to comfort herself. Maybe she trailed her fingers across the patterned wallpaper? The repetitions in the pattern soothe her, keep her company. Like a friend who always returns.

She's just moved to Stockholm. She has walked home early from one of the many society gatherings she's been invited to. Why does she feel lonelier among all these people than she does when she sits alone in her study, absorbed in her mathematics?

She can't sleep, so she gets up again and walks barefoot across the cold stone floor. She sits down at the desk and lights the paraffin lamp. But she's too tired to do any mathematics. Instead, she writes a letter to her friend Marie Mendelson, whom she got to know during a stay in Paris:

> At present, I play the role of comforting, compassionate sister. I find myself in a society where I am surrounded by people who occupy themselves with things in which I have little interest, but who are struggling with greater and lesser challenges that require my moral support. The worst of it is that I know I'm unable to give them sufficient help.

Why did Sofia settle in Stockholm if she wasn't happy there? Was the relationship with Weierstrass over? Did it hurt to be in the same city as him? Was that why she fled Berlin? Or did she perhaps leave Berlin because she knew there was no academic future for her there? No self-respecting university would appoint a female professor. After completing her doctorate in 1874, the only offer of employment she received was to teach mathematics at a primary school in Russia. "My ability to recite the multiplication tables is, unfortunately, rather weak," she noted. Only in 1883 was she finally offered a professorship at the university in Stockholm.

Sofia's closest friend in Stockholm was the Swedish author Anne Charlotte Leffler, sister of the mathematician Gösta Mittag-Leffler. In the biography she published in the year after Sofia's death, Anne Charlotte wrote that Sofia was a natural focal point in social settings, because she had "the natural-born poet's deep human compassion for all of life's conflicts, even the most trivial." People found her to be obliging and unpretentious, kind, thoughtful, and empathetic to those farther down the social ladder. Her desire to please others gave her a sympathetic air that charmed everyone around her. But in reality, she was reserved by nature, and let few people get truly close. According to Anne Charlotte, Sofia was extremely restrained when it came to sharing her deepest emotions, especially her sorrows.

Although Sofia became a popular figure in Stockholm's social circles, she never felt truly at home there. She longed for discussions that took surprising twists and turns, that required agile leaps of thought, preferably one-on-one. Instead, she was drawn into conversations about everyday trifles. People began to come to her for advice on anything and everything, from which dress they should wear to marital problems. "It seems as if the trend-setting women of Stockholm have astonishingly few interesting and exciting topics of conversation, so it appears a good deed to give them something to talk about," she wrote in a letter.

But at the same time, she expressed her concern that the newspapers might dig into her past and find something unfavorable to write about:

Now that my name has begun to appear in various news-
papers and weeklies, I live in constant fear that they will dig up
something that may harm me. Through acquaintances I have
requested that, as a personal favor to me, all the editors of
the biggest newspapers refrain from writing about me until I
have given them permission to do so. The newspapers here are
very fair, and have complied with my request, with the exception
of two small and insignificant publications.

OH, SOFIA. WHAT was it from your past that you wished to hide? The rumors of a romantic relationship with Weierstrass?

Did you struggle with the feeling that you were putting on an act? That other people were forming an idealized image of you, one that you felt you had to try and live up to? Did you fear that nobody would like you if they found out who you really were? What you had once been capable of doing?

Did you long to be free of having to always be so sensible? To be able to do something terribly wrong, and yet still be loved?

Perhaps your yearning for Weierstrass became too much, and you started to meet again in secret? Was it because of him that you cut short your summer vacation in Norway in 1886?

You and Anne Charlotte were supposed to visit Alexander Kielland in Stavanger. You'd been looking forward to it for months and had already gotten to know Jonas Lie and Edvard Grieg in Paris. But on a steamer in Telemark, you suddenly decided to abandon your trip. The excuse you gave was that an irresistible mathematical idea had just occurred to you, and you simply had to spend the summer investigating it. You then took the first steamer back to Christiania, leaving your friend to continue the planned journey alone.

Did you seek out the same wholeness and unity in love as in your intellectual life? Just as your mind aspired to absolute clarity and truth, your heart likely aspired to the ultimate love. When someone piqued your interest, you turned your undivided attention on this person and lost all appetite for everything else. Of you, Anne Charlotte wrote:

> *She was endlessly giving and bestowed abundant sympathy; she lavished us with small proofs of her friendship and was ever poised to make any self-sacrifice. But she expected the same in return, to feel that she meant just as much to the other as that person meant to her.*

THERE IS A letter from the Labor and Welfare Administration in the mailbox. Rakel has been summoned to another meeting. Payments of her work assessment allowance will stop during the summer, when she reaches the maximum time limit. And she'll remain ineligible for disability benefits until they can be sure that her condition is permanent—that she will never be well again.

Her caseworker says there's no point in applying for disability until all appropriate measures have been tried. Rakel hasn't yet participated in the "Active Days" exercise scheme, nor has she completed "The Process." The woman recommends that Rakel complete "The Process" as soon as possible. It takes just three days, and by the end of it over ninety percent of the participants feel well again.

The course costs 15,000 kroner, and she must pay this fee herself. The reason it's so expensive is that participants will be much more motivated to get well when they've paid such a high price for it. But you can only apply for a place in the course if you're free of skepticism. You must have complete faith that you'll get better. And if you don't get better, then it's nobody's fault but your own. You must have misunderstood something, or have been too skeptical. It's strictly forbidden to reveal details of the contents of the course to outsiders. By submitting your application, you confirm that you have read and accepted these terms and conditions.

She has no choice. All she can do is try to set aside all doubt and believe that this will work. It would be fantastic if the course could make her well again! She's already imagining all the things she could do. Write a novel. Have children. Start teaching again.

The English woman leading the course has set her chair in the center of the semicircle of participants. She asks everyone to spend thirty seconds looking for red objects in the room. Afterward, everyone is to close their eyes and try to remember what they saw. Between them, the members of the group remember an impressive number of items. But then the woman asks whether, without opening their eyes, they can name any blue objects in the room. A quiet falls over them.

Rakel imagines the room, and answers that the wastepaper basket is blue. And that there was also something blue up on the shelf—some ring binders, perhaps. There was a blue pen on the desk, and wasn't the woman closest to the window wearing a blue sweater too? Rakel gets the impression that the course leader is becoming irritated with her. It clearly wasn't her intention that anyone should answer, because this exercise was supposed to show them that they only see what they focus on, to the exclusion of everything else. So when they focus on the fact that they are sick, they ignore all the signs that show them that they are, on the contrary, healthy.

Afterward, they do an exercise where they walk in square movements across the floor, learning to replace negative thoughts with positive ones. But Rakel can't escape the fatigue. The other participants, though, seem to feel better. Her eyes fill with tears.

"That's it, *now* you're in the right place—you might just get something out of this course after all," says the woman. "Are you willing to do whatever it takes to get well?" Rakel nods.

The woman turns to face the group again. "The first thing you need to do is use this exercise to reprogram your brain, so that it understands that you are actually healthy. If you go around looking for symptoms of illness all the time, your brain will believe that you're ill. You must ignore the signals from your body. This will eventually allow the neural pathways in your brain to be reprogrammed, and you will become well."

The woman tells a story to convince the group that it's possible to think oneself into good health. She tells them about the time a priest was supposed to visit a prison inmate who was ill with cancer. The prisoner was so sick that he was on his deathbed; the priest was called to perform last rites. But the priest made a mistake. He went into a neighboring cell and performed last rites on a healthy inmate instead. When this prisoner received the last rites, he believed he must be ill and died in his cell that same night. But the prisoner with cancer got better, because he hadn't received the last rites after all.

Why doesn't the Labor and Welfare Administration require that cancer patients take this course instead of going through radiation and chemotherapy? Rakel wonders.

But then the fact that she's had a skeptical thought terrifies her. Imagine if she doesn't get well again because she's too disbelieving. She forces herself not to be skeptical when the woman ends the course by asking the participants to sign a document on which they must check a box to affirm that they are well. It is important that they all complete the document, because it will be used in research into the effectiveness of the treatment.

If they *really* want to get better, they must check the box to state that they are well, the course leader explains. And the prerequisite for getting well is that from this point forward, they must always say that they are well—both to themselves and to others. Because although they may not be feeling one hundred percent just yet, they'll get well eventually, as long as they say it enough times and refrain from thinking skeptical thoughts. The reprogramming of the brain can take time.

Rakel does her best. She does the square exercise hundreds of times every day, ignoring the signals from her body. She takes walks to Kringstadsetra, even though she feels as if she's going to faint, and reads books with a splitting headache. But after a month she's so unwell that she collapses on the living-room floor. She throws up everything she tries to eat, spikes a fever of 104, and is bedridden for weeks. She's so dizzy that she crawls along the floor when she needs to use the bathroom.

What if it's her own fault that she's still ill? If it's because she hasn't done her best? And when summer comes, her benefits will run out. What will she live on then? She can manage as long as she has Mamma and Pappa, but she doesn't have the strength for this life without them.

Current age: 37 years

Expected average lifetime: 87 years

Estimated average time not confined to bed until death: 4 percent, or $^1/_{25}$

Calculated ratio: 1 active year per 25 bedridden years

She therefore has $(87-37)/25 = 2$ active years of her life remaining.

And 48 confined to her bed.

HOW PLEASANT DEATH must be for those who are weary of life! Rakel lies in bed listening to the radio. NRK Alltid Klassisk is playing *Vier Ernste Gesänge* by Brahms, *Four Serious Songs*. With texts from the Bible. An old recording with bass singer Alexander Kipnis. She's never spent much time listening to Brahms, even though she likes his Cello Sonata in E Minor. But now it's as if Kipnis's deep voice rocks her. Tenderly, warmly, soothingly. As if it wants to show her that pain can be smelted into art.

O Tod, wie wohl tust du!

She understands the text so well. She's had enough of life herself. Life, which never stops kicking people's feet out from under them, in order to see whether they're still capable of living. And which continues to kick them long after they're down. Natural selection. Survival of the fittest. Come to think of it, it's quite astonishing that her inept genes didn't get wiped out long ago.

But then it happens again, in the final verse. The way that she can *hear* the light:

Nun aber bleibet Glaube, Hoffnung, Liebe, diese drei;
Aber die Liebe ist die größte unter ihnen.

So they remain, these three: faith, hope, and love.
But the greatest among them is love.

The radio host says that this was the last cycle of songs Brahms composed before he died; at the time his great love, the pianist Clara Schumann, was dying. Rakel is puzzled. Clara was married to Robert Schumann—did she have a relationship with Brahms too?

She takes the biography of Johannes Brahms from where it has stood, untouched on the bookcase, since she bought it many years ago. Brahms is just twenty years old when, in 1853, he meets Clara and Robert Schumann for the first time. Armed with a letter of recommendation from the violinist Joseph Joachim, he shows up unannounced at their home in order to play a few pieces he's composed.

Robert Schumann is so inspired by Brahms's talent that he describes him as "the new Beethoven, the one everyone has been waiting for." He publishes an article about Brahms in the magazine *Neue Zeitschrift für Musik*, making the young Brahms famous all across Germany. In her diary, Clara writes of Brahms:

> It seems as if he has been sent to us straight from God. He played
> sonatas and scherzos for us, which he had composed himself, and
> all of them exhibited an effervescent imagination, great depth of
> feeling, and a masterful command of form. . . . He has a great
> future ahead of him, because his genius will only truly come into
> its own when he begins to compose for the orchestra.

Clara is fourteen years older than Brahms and has been married to Robert Schumann for thirteen years. They are expecting their eighth child together.

But Brahms dreams of Clara all the same. In her, he has found a kindred spirit, someone with whom he can share his deepest interests and visions. He sends her the pieces of music he composes, in order to receive criticism and feedback—and he dedicates most of these pieces to her. But he feels a deep conflict between his love for Clara and his affection for his benefactor, Robert Schumann. He feels such despair that he considers taking his own life.

Most of the letters exchanged between the two were burned, but from the few that remain it is clear that Brahms had romantic feelings for Clara. There is a sincerity in Brahms's letters. Although they're mostly about music, it is the few lines in which he addresses Clara directly that contain the most beautiful poetry. He calls her "innigst geliebte Freundin," "most sincerely beloved friend." In one of his letters to her, he writes:

> My beloved Clara, if only I could write as tenderly as I love you, and do as many loving and tender acts for you as I would wish. You are so exceptionally dear to me that I am unable to express it. I could ceaselessly call you beloved and so many other things without ever becoming tired of giving you compliments. . . . Your letters are like kisses to me.

When Robert Schumann is admitted to a mental hospital following a suicide attempt in 1854, Brahms moves into the uppermost floor of the house where Clara lives, to support her through this difficult time and help her take care of the children. But after Robert Schumann dies in July 1856 at just forty-six years old, Brahms moves out of the house again. Clara is hurt and writes in her diary: "My heart bleeds. It feels as if I have just returned from a funeral."

In a letter to Joseph Joachim three years after Robert Schumann's death, Brahms writes these words about Clara:

> I think that I not only respect and admire her; I love her and am spellbound by her. Often, and with great effort, I only just manage to stop myself from silently embracing her. I don't know, it feels so natural that I do not think she would be offended by it.

Brahms and Clara maintain their close friendship for the rest of their lives. They spend the summers near each other, and in 1868 they set out on a concert tour to Vienna together, and later to England and Holland. Brahms never marries. None of the younger women he meets inspires him in the way that Clara does. In 1896, just a few weeks before Clara dies, Brahms writes these lines to her:

> *If you believe the worst may be expected, you must grant me a*
> *few words so that I may come and see your dear eyes while they*
> *remain open. For with them, so much will close for me.*

He only just makes it in time for her funeral, and dies himself just a few months later at the age of sixty-three.

The saddest things in life are also the most beautiful. Rakel thinks it was the longing for Clara that inspired the most beautiful music in Schumann and Brahms. It's as if she can hear their love and pain in the music. Even though it is mainly childhood memories that Schumann evokes in his composition Kinderszenen from 1838, it's probably Clara he dreams of in the most famous of the pieces: *Träumerei*.

RAKEL HAS DISCOVERED that there are several variants of Rubik's cube in addition to the usual version with 3×3×3 pieces. Not only are there larger versions with 4×4×4 pieces and 5×5×5 pieces, there are also variants that aren't cube-shaped, but instead shaped like an octahedron, a dodecahedron, or an icosahedron. It's as if a new world opens up to her—yet another of these spaces she never knew existed.

There are people out there in the world who modify the cubes by hand. And not only do they modify the cubes' appearance; they also modify the internal mechanism in ways that make the cubes function differently, transforming them into new challenges to solve. She becomes a member of an online forum for people interested in Rubik's cubes and other similar puzzles.

She notices him right away. Recognizes the music in his language. And to think that his name is David—it's as if he's the real-life version of the boy she always dreamed of. But *she* doesn't contact *him*. It's David who contacts her after she writes her first post on the forum. But once they have begun to correspond, it's she who's the most eager. Although he's the one who writes the longest letters. It takes her several days to compose a brief email, but she has plenty of time.

David tells her about his hobby—creating special types of puzzles that can take the form of small works of art. At the moment he's working on a chess set whose board constitutes the lid of a chest. By moving the chess pieces in a certain order, the chest's locking mechanism is released so that the lid opens. The chest is then transformed into a music box, which plays melodies from the musical *Chess*.

The problem is that the locking mechanism only works when there are a maximum of twelve pieces on the board. And in a game of chess there are thirty-two pieces. Rakel asks him whether he's considered creating a simpler version. The starting position on the board could be the position of the pieces after fifty-five moves in the thirteenth game of the World Chess Championship between Spassky and Fisher in 1972. And the moves to open the box could reflect the rest of the endgame, initiated by Spassky's elegant h5, which creates a free pawn on the g-file.

David is excited by the idea. He throws himself into the work and sends her updates as he goes along. The construction of the clockwork in the music box. The bifurcated steel comb with seventy-two teeth of varying lengths, tuned to the notes of the musical scale. The brass cylinder with studs that set the metal teeth vibrating, and the spring, air brake, and regulator.

But he's struggling with the locking mechanism for the lid and its interaction with the movements of the chess pieces. The mechanism has a tendency to get stuck, and the situation worsens as the number of moves increases. He currently has to limit the solution to ten moves and set the starting position to that after Fischer promoted his pawn to a queen on h1 in his sixty-fourth move. But he has several ideas about how he can improve the mechanism.

She enjoys how he describes the details of the process to her, how he experiments with different techniques in order to achieve the desired result. It makes her feel as if she's joining him on a voyage of discovery, even though all she does is lie in bed. She listens to the music in his speech more closely. It's like the thing that she fell for in Jakob's voice. If only she could permit herself, perhaps she might be able to love David.

If there's anyone else out there for her other than Jakob, it must be David. It would help to know that it's possible to love someone other than Jakob. Because if there's one more person here in the world she can have such feelings for, then it would be easier to believe that there might be others too. That Jakob is not the only one. In the arithmetic of the heart, the difference between one and two is like the difference between one and infinity.

And anyway, David lives on the other side of the world. It can't do any harm to love him, even though his forum profile hints that he might be married. They're never going to meet. She's too ill for that.

HER LETTERS GRADUALLY get longer. Writing to David is like writing to herself. Because he sees the detail in everything around him, just as she does. Because he understands what she means. She sees things more clearly when she sees them with him.

Dear David!

You have excellent taste in problems! Your puzzles are some of the most original I've seen. I used to think that puzzles were used up once they had been solved, but yours really are miniature works of art that can be enjoyed for a long time. Their simplicity, elegance, and creativity—and how you combine things in unexpected ways—give them a special kind of beauty. The same allure that's found in a beautiful mathematical proof.

Sometimes I wonder whether my whole life has been a singular quest for beauty. Beauty in mathematics, and beauty in literature and in music. I feel that creating mathematics and writing fiction are closely related. While authors are poets in the universe of language, mathematicians seek the poetry in the language of the universe. The German mathematician Karl Weierstrass once wrote that any great mathematician must also be a poet. When I was young, several people told me that I'd be a poet when I grew up. So in a way, it feels as if I've tried to investigate whether the reverse implication is true: whether every poet must also be a great mathematician. I still don't know the answer, but I doubt that this is the case.

Over the past few years, I've started to dream of writing a novel. I've marveled at how the enjoyment of hearing a piece of music often gets stronger the better you know the piece, while a novel rarely has the same impact on third reading. Is it because music relies on recognition, while literature relies on the unexpected? Or has it more to do with the structure of the music, how the themes reflect each other so that the listener discovers ever new connections? The way the interplay of colors in a painting can fluctuate in different light, so that the painting continually changes? If so, it must be possible to write a novel in the same way. A novel that gets richer every time you read it, because you discover new connections that were previously invisible. A novel that carries something of the eternal beauty of music and mathematics within it.

One of the most alluring things about mathematics is perhaps the feeling of being able to uncover unshakeable truths. And that terms such as truth and beauty obtain a kind of objectivity, because mathematicians have a shared understanding of what constitutes a valid proof and what is aesthetically beautiful. The disadvantage is that the truths of mathematics don't say anything about what is true in the world beyond mathematics itself.
Rakel

David asks whether it's possible for nonmathematicians to glimpse the beauty in mathematics. She sends him a picture of her favorite fractal. A few weeks later, she receives a parcel in the mail. David has painstakingly worked the fractal into a puzzle, and he would very much like to create more puzzles with her. She comes up with ideas for what he can make; he figures out how the ideas can be realized and executes the laborious work with a perfectionist's patience.

One of the puzzles is shaped like a treble clef attached to a violin. The aim is to release the clef, so that the violin's lid can be opened. The violin box is then transformed into a music box, which plays the Violin Sonata by César Franck. Another is shaped like a boy who is sharing his balloon with a little girl. The aim is to pass the string of the balloon from his hand to hers. As you solve the puzzle, pieces that block the string's path have to be pushed aside, forming a passage in the shape of a heart.

DAVID'S BIRTHDAY IS in early September. She sends him a video greeting from a summer vacation long ago, in which she's balancing on a slack line while holding her hands behind her back and solving a Rubik's cube she can't see. She knows that he's fascinated by such stunts, that he appreciates the effort that lies behind them.

"Incredible. You make it look so easy. You must have great balance," David writes.

She tells him about the feeling in her body after the first step she took on the line without losing her balance. The feeling of having made a completely pure movement, a pure weight transfer forward, purer than any other movement she had ever made in her life. How walking on a slack line is a kind of meditation. Like juggling with five balls when you've finally mastered it and can concentrate on keeping the pattern flowing instead of focusing on each individual throw.

David sends her a video of him juggling two balls in one hand while he solves a Rubik's cube in the other. She plays the video over and over again, in order to study the trick more closely. But most of all, to study David. His mouth. His hands. There's something about David that makes you notice him, makes you want to get to know him. His dark, curly hair and the rounded shape of his face. His childish features, which make him look younger than he really is. Something alert and youthful in the way he moves his body, the way he gesticulates when he speaks.

She tells him about the juggling pattern she made up many years ago. A variation of Mills Mess inspired by Rubenstein's Revenge, but where the balls are moved in an S-shaped orbit. It's hard to explain over email, so she sends him a video Jakob took of her, showing how the pattern is juggled.

She explains that juggling the opposite way, using bouncy balls against the floor, is a comfortable way of juggling. It's actually easier to juggle five balls by bouncing them against the floor than it is by throwing them up into the air. It's a lot less work, because you only need to give the balls a little nudge in the right direction, and then gravity does the rest.

But you need bouncy balls with at least eighty percent rebound. Silicon balls are the best. They're velvety soft in the hands. And once you've experienced such a ball in the hand, you may never want to play with any others.

"I couldn't help but notice the scar on your left elbow," David writes. "Did something bad happen?"

"Yes, I played the violin," she answers.

"Oh, you *fought* the violin," he writes.

She tells him how she developed tendonitis in high school, because she'd had to play five concerts in one week and practiced intensively in a room that was far too cold. It never got better, and after two years she needed surgery. She regards this as the first time she had her heart broken. Because a violinist was what she'd always wanted to be. Ever since she'd heard César Franck's Violin Sonata for the very first time.

"I thought you said your hair was brown, but it's most definitely black," David teases.

"According to my childhood passport, my hair is actually dark blond," she answers. She tells David how Pappa had taken her to the police station to order her a passport. The man behind the counter had cast a glance at her hair and said: "I think we'll put black for her hair color."

Pappa had given the man a stern look and replied, "No, it's more like dark blond."

"And the officer simply accepted that?" David asks.

"My father can be very persuasive," she answers. "I really wanted to blend in with the other Norwegian children, and not having my hair described as black was the main thing I obsessed about."

"I suppose your father insisted that you're blue-eyed too?" David jokes.

She tells him that in her passport her eye color is given as brown.

"But your eyes are hazel," David writes.

Rakel feels warm inside. He's noticed the color of her eyes. She doesn't know exactly what the word *hazel* means, but it's nice to finally have a name to put to her eye color.

Jakob has told her that they're neither brown nor green, but green at their outermost edges, with a brown core surrounding the pupils, and streaks of gold. But there isn't a name for this eye color in Norwegian. That's why Jakob simply called her the girl with the golden eyes: "The most beautiful eyes in the world, that gild everything and everyone you look at."

SOFIA WAS HAPPIEST when she was completely absorbed in her work. In such periods she was effervescent and full of life, sparkling and alert, bursting with ideas and enterprise. In Stockholm, she missed having someone who could light mathematical sparks within her in the way that Europe's greatest mathematicians—Weierstrass, Hermite, and Poincaré—could do. But she found a literary collaborator in Anne Charlotte Leffler. Together, they wrote the play *Kampen för Lyckan, The Struggle for Happiness*. Sofia came up with ideas for the characters and plot, and Anne Charlotte undertook the painstaking work of getting the lines down on paper. In a letter to a friend, she describes the enthusiasm they both felt for this work:

> *Sofia is overjoyed at this new turn life has taken; she says that she only now understands how a man always falls in love with the mother of his children for a second time. And I am naturally the mother, since it is I who will bring this child into the world. She is so full of affection for me that it makes me happy just to see the radiant glances she casts my way. . . .*
>
> *Never before have I felt such great enthusiasm for an idea. As soon as Sofia shared it with me, it struck me like a bolt of lightning striking a lightning conductor. Yes, it truly was an explosion. . . .*

You likely think that we are just a couple of overgrown children, the pair of us, and yes, thank God—that's exactly what we are. Luckily there is a kingdom that is better than all the kingdoms of the earth, to which we have the keys—the kingdom of the imagination, where whoever wishes to be so can be a ruler, and where all matters are shaped exactly as one pleases.

Sofia's idea was to tell two parallel stories using the same characters and setting, the first time as it happened in reality, and the second time the way things *might have been*, if only the characters in the play had made different choices at a critical moment. One of the protagonists, Alice, seems to express Sofia's innermost longings:

I am so used to people loving others more than they love me. At school, they said that I was the most gifted. But I always knew that it was an irony of fate to have been given so many gifts, only for me to feel even more intensely what I might have been to others when nobody wanted me. . . .

I do not ask for much—so little—only that no other person must always stand in the way and get closer. This is the only thing I have longed for in my entire life, to be another person's first choice. . . . Just once, let me show you what I can be when someone truly loves me. . . . Look at me closely. Am I pretty? Yes, when someone loves me, I am pretty. Otherwise, I am not. Am I good? Yes, when someone loves me, I am kindheartedness itself. Am I unselfish? Oh, I can be so selfless that any of my thoughts may dissolve into the thought of another.

Anne Charlotte writes that she had never seen Sofia so happy, so radiant with joy, as she was during this time:

At the end of the working day we took long walks in the forest close to the district in which we both lived, and here she would run

253

across stones and hillocks, taking me in her arms and dancing, shouting that life was glorious and the future enchanting—full of promise.

But for her part, Anne Charlotte eventually feels a need to concentrate on her writing in peace and quiet:

I have now introduced a small change to our working method. To Sofia's great distress I have forbidden her from accessing my study until I have completed the writing of the entire second act. I have been far too disturbed and agitated by our perpetual collaboration during the first act. I have lost perspective and the intense internal sense of cohabitation with the characters. . . . All my soul's happiness lies in its lonely work, and for me this is the great drawback of a collaboration, even with such a kindred spirit as Sofia. In this area she is my complete opposite; she is Alice (in The Struggle for Happiness), who is in fact unable to create, unable to comprehend anything with all of her soul when she is unable to share it with another.

Sofia dreams of continuing the literary collaboration. But Anne Charlotte, who feels a growing urge to reconquer herself, to again become the sole ruler of her thoughts and feelings, decides to travel to Italy. There, she meets the great love of her life, the mathematician Pasquale del Pezzo, Duke of Caianello.

When Sofia receives the news that her friend has found love, she writes:

What a happy child of the sun you are! To have found such a great, deep, and mutual love at your age is truly a fate worthy only of a blessed child like you. But it was long ago decided that of the two of us it is you who are Happiness, while I am and surely will only ever remain the Struggle.

DAVID TELLS HER that there is something called the International Puzzle Party, which is held every summer. It's a private event that only specially invited guests may attend. All the great puzzle experts participate, such as Donald Knuth and Martin Gardner. But to ensure that outsiders can't sneak in, the gathering is kept so secret that participants aren't even allowed to tell outsiders in which city the event will take place until it's all over. The only detail made public is that the event is held by turns in Europe, the United States, and Japan. And next year the event will be in Europe, in Berlin. David knows many of the participants and thinks he can manage to get her in if she's interested.

Imagine being able to meet him in reality after all. *Of course* she's interested. But she doesn't know whether she's strong enough to make the journey. David sends her the draft of a puzzle he's hoping to be able to give to her in Berlin. It's shaped like a sparrow, with three mathematical symbols in its beak. A negation symbol, an existential quantifier, and a universal quantifier. The aim is to release the symbols by feeding them through the bird's labyrinth-shaped gut. When they emerge on the other side, they are turned on their heads to become the letters L, E, and A. As if the little sparrow transforms mathematics into literature. The story of Lea and Rakel.

Little Sparrow—it flashes through her. It's as if David not only sees her in the present, but that he also sees all the past lives she might have lived, the people she may have been. Sofia Kovalevskaya has also been to Berlin. That's where she met Weierstrass.

SHE STARTS TO dream about the days in Berlin. How she enters the hotel reception on the first day. Perhaps David is already standing there, talking to a small group of people. He catches sight of her at once.

"Excuse me, there's someone I need to see," he says to the others. Then he comes straight toward her, his expression just as open and happy as she has imagined it will be.

"Rachel!" he cries, throwing his arms wide in greeting.

She has to stop herself from casting her arms around his neck.

"Come here," he says, reaching for her. She can enter his embrace if she takes just a couple of steps closer. "Everyone knows anyway."

What does everyone know? she wonders. But then she understands his meaning. There's no reason to pretend that she doesn't.

She simply walks into his open arms and presses her body against his, linking them together from head to toe, burrowing her face into the soft skin at the base of his throat, pressing her lips to his neck in what she doesn't realize are tiny kisses—until she senses that he's wondering whether what he can feel at the base of his throat are tiny kisses—and then she just sets her lips silently against his skin, moving them slightly, so that he might think that what he just felt were natural movements, that this is how Rakel's lips usually behave.

His breathing calms. Long, heavy breaths. Her breaths match the rhythm of his, as if they're one and the same organism. In and out, in and out, in and out. By breathing so slowly he makes time pass more slowly, his embrace last longer. She thinks she's never breathed so slowly before. And never before have three inbreaths and three outbreaths contained so much.

David. She imagines his mouth. It's the first mouth she's ever seen that has made her want to taste it straightaway. With Jakob it was different. *He* had asked for permission to kiss *her*. She had never looked at his mouth and thought that there was anything special about it.

She imagines David's hands too. His lively but confident hands. And his serious eyes, which change color when he smiles. This combination of depth and simplicity that she likes so well, of seriousness and playfulness. His ability to get completely absorbed in something. The calm in his voice—a voice in which she can find rest. And the first thing she noticed: the music in his speech, the way he writes. This mixture of wisdom and a sense of humor, which seems to be common to the people she falls for. Something about them that makes her want to sit at their feet and listen to their voice forever.

RAKEL HAS ALWAYS believed that she must be the most sentimental person on earth, but now it seems she's met her match. David has offered to repair a rare type of Rubik's cube she bought but that turned out to be broken when she received it in the mail. He has the same type of cube himself and says that, after cobbling together the broken parts of hers, he would like to keep her cube and send her the one that's in perfect condition.

She thinks he's doing this to be nice and replies that she can't possibly accept such a generous offer. His cube is worth far more than hers.

Then he explains that he really would prefer to keep the cube he's repaired for her because it has a story. The fact that he received it in the mail from her. That he's opened it and seen it from the inside. That he's painstakingly put the pieces back together again. And since he has no plans ever to sell this particular cube, its personal value is far more important to him than its actual sales value.

She discovers that his sentimentality must be infectious, because when she thinks about it, she realizes that the stories attached to objects mean far more than their monetary value to her too. And she knows that she's already found the answer to the question she once asked herself. She knows that she loves David. And that she therefore has to stop writing to him.

SHE CAN'T SEEM to stop writing to David. She continues to write long emails to him every week. The only difference is that she no longer sends them to him. The messages from David gradually become more and more infrequent, as if he's about to forget. David doesn't need Rakel. He has a busy family life, with kids and a wife who love him. Why has Rakel been equipped with so much love if there's nobody out there in need of it?

Other people have a life. They forget. They don't lie under the covers like her, collecting moments. Yet again, she's just a tiny morsel of someone else's life—while he's almost her entire world. Why does she think that people love her more than they actually do? Because she loves them so much? Because love believes and trusts in everything?

Has she simply let herself be fooled this entire time? Has Jakob never loved her? Is it possible to love two women at the same time in such a way that the love for one of them strengthens the love for the other? Either because you love the same qualities in both women, or because of the contrasts between them? Maybe he was right when he said that he didn't know what it means to love. The most important thing is that she has loved him. She won't have to die having never truly loved. *If equal affection cannot be, let the more loving one be me.*

So she's experienced all too well how love believes and trusts in everything. But can love also forgive everything? Can you be forgiven for sins you're unable to regret? If you know with your entire being that you would do it all over again? That if you were to permit yourself a single sin here in this life, this is the sin you would choose?

Can she ever hope for forgiveness? Will she ever be able to forgive herself? She *knew* that what she was doing was wrong. She, who had never even snatched an apple as a child because she couldn't make herself do something she knew wasn't right. She, who has always possessed the ability to understand the situations of others, to feel their suffering as her own. She should have been able to resist the temptation. Now she feels like an off-key note in the musical score of the universe.

The point is not to play all the notes correctly, Rakel. The point is to impart the universe's symphony.

You were born to be expanded, just as the universe is expanding. Ever since you were born, you have been growing. At first, everyone can see this, but after a while it happens more subtly, and you yourself must find the things that expand you. The colors. The books. The people. Everything in the universe expands and is expanded by forces beyond itself.

You were born to evolve. And you evolve most through encounters with others. And love is the only way you can truly weave yourself in and out of another person. It's the tentacles of the fractal. It trusts and believes in everything. But it will also teach you about forgiveness.

WITHOUT JAKOB'S GAZE, she no longer knows who she is.

She thinks about God. The greater the number of words, the more distant he becomes—if she's going to find him, she'll have to look in the little things. She's sure about that. Because in the beginning there was only one word. "In the beginning was the Word, and the Word was God." It must have been easier to catch sight of him back then.

Maybe the reason she's never found God is that people's words have diminished him for her. She's always felt he must be bigger than this if he exists. More tolerant. Someone who doesn't condemn people to eternal damnation on the grounds of which religion they grew up with. That he must be someone who unites instead of divides.

Perhaps he actually exists in a higher dimension. If so, God as he's projected down into our own dimension might look different depending on where you are. And the various depictions of him might come from each narrator's independent point of view, even though they seem contradictory. Maybe you have to collect all the pieces in order to get a sense of the greater whole.

Like when a three-dimensional pyramid in space is projected down onto a single plane. A two-dimensional being living on the base plane will claim that the pyramid is a square. An equivalent being living on a plane parallel to one of the lateral surfaces will claim that the pyramid is a triangle. From other planes it may look like a rectangle, a parallelogram, or a trapezium. The two-dimensional beings would argue among themselves, because it seems impossible that the object can be a square, triangle, rectangle, parallelogram, and trapezium all at once. They would be willing to go to war for their truth—because they're unaware that a higher dimension exists where all their descriptions can be true at the same time. That there is a greater world that encompasses their world along with many others.

Perhaps we've been created with this need to take a bite of the forbidden apple? Maybe God has planted the sin within us so that we'll be able to find him? You don't find God until you search for him. And you don't search for God until you need him, need his forgiveness. Perhaps the great Composer wished for his symphony to be more minor than major, that the disharmony, the wrong notes, leads to something greater. A greater harmony.

Maybe it's not only love that is like a fractal. Perhaps the universe itself has a fractal structure. That you are reborn as ever new copies of yourself, only with a slight twist. That you are given the chance to try again and again, until you find out who you really are. Until you find your true musical key. Then you'll have reached your nirvana, the keynote where you can rest. Your true paradise. It's magnanimous of the great Composer to give us the chance to try and fail, that we're permitted to make the wrong choices before we find the right ones. That even the most minuscule particle of dust in the universe carries a copy of the entire universe within it. *But the human heart remains the same all through the ages.*

She starts looking for connections in the universe, reads Chinese astrology for the first time in her life. The circle of the Chinese zodiac, with its twelve animals. According to the Chinese astrologists, because she was born in the year of the Tiger, she will get along best with those who were born in the year of the Dog or the year of the Horse. She thinks about the people she's most fond of out of everyone she's ever met. David was born in the autumn of 1970, the year of the Dog. So far, so good for the theory. But Jakob was born in 1955, and that's the year of the Goat. So the theory doesn't work after all, even with her tiny sample of two people.

But then she discovers it—the space between the Western calendar and the Chinese calendar. The fact that the Chinese year doesn't start until February. And Jakob was born in January. He was born in this space. He was born in the year of the Horse after all. She thinks of her old high-school teacher. He too was born in the year of the Horse, but in an earlier cycle than Jakob. She checks Lea's date of birth, as if she wants to see it in black and white that she would be a better fit for Jakob herself. But Lea was born in the year of the Dog. She's just as good a match for Jakob.

She tests the theory on more people. Sofia was born in 1850, and that was the year of the Dog. Weierstrass was born in 1815, and that was the year of the Pig. Dogs and pigs aren't suited to each other. No wonder Sofia was unhappy. According to Chinese astrology, she would have been better off with Gösta Mittag-Leffler, who was born in the year of the Horse.

Clara was born in 1819, and that was the year of the Rabbit. Rabbits get along best with sheep and pigs. But Schumann was born in the year of the Horse, and Brahms in the year of the Snake. Of course they were unhappy, all three of them. Clara should probably have paired up with Joseph Joachim, who was born in the year of the Rabbit, like her.

MAYBE HAPPINESS LIES in immortalizing the golden moments, in bringing them out over and over, in order to bask in their glow. So that those moments never die, but instead are given eternal life. Become the very thing you look back on as your life on the day you stand on the threshold of eternity and turn to cast a last glance at yourself from that outermost perspective. Perhaps it is only then that you'll answer the great Composer's question about which key you walk in. That the Composer will give you the freedom to decide that your key is A major, even though it might seem that you spent most of your life walking around in A minor. If happiness is the ability to let yourself be fulfilled by the luminous moments, one day she will manage to be happy.

SOFIA WAS ONLY eighteen years old when she entered into a marriage of convenience with paleontologist Vladimir Kovalevsky, so she would have the opportunity to study abroad. The plan had actually been that Vladimir would marry Anyuta, and the couple would then take Sofia with them upon leaving the country. But after having met both sisters, Vladimir refused to go through with the original plan. He favored Sofia over her sister and asked to marry her instead. In a letter to his brother, he wrote:

> My Little Sparrow is such a wonderful creature that I will not describe her, because you would only believe that I am spellbound. . . . I cannot hide from myself the fact that she is a thousand times better, wiser, and more talented than me. She is actually quite the phenomenon, and I cannot comprehend how fate could send her my way.

In her youth, Sofia had developed the notion that the highest and most noble form of love was platonic affection. Her dream for the future was a silent interdependence, where the two lovers immersed themselves in scientific study side by side. "Hereafter, I will call you Brother," she wrote in one of her first letters to Vladimir. And a few months after the wedding, she wrote to her sister:

Brother is very courteous and charming, and I am truly attached to him, even though our friendship has naturally lost all trace of joyous expectation. You would not believe how attentive he is toward me, how he waits upon me and is ready to suppress all his own needs and yield to mine. I feel terribly ashamed to be so deeply indebted to him: I truly love him with all my soul, but only as one loves a younger brother. I would be extremely sad if he were to learn that there is anything in our life with which I am dissatisfied, so I am completely dependent upon you, Anyuta, not giving him so much as a hint of this when you next see him. Because I am solely dissatisfied with myself, dissatisfied without reason. And when it comes to platonic love, everything has fallen into place in my favor. But without you, Anyuta, I cannot live.

Sofia's friend Julia Lermontova commented on the relationship between Sofia and her husband in the period that followed their wedding:

She lived hand in hand with a man who loved her with a restrained passion, and it seemed that she treated him with the same tenderness. Both apparently continued to live in ignorance of the painfully irrevocable passion that is usually called love.

A year later, the situation had changed. The couple were no longer living under the same roof. Vladimir wrote to his brother that he loved Sofia deeply, but that he was unable to live with her nevertheless:

In both my personality and in my work I am, deep down, a nomad and wanderer. I would be deeply unhappy were I to feel myself bound to any fixed place. . . .

She is a person one must take care of, like a child. She is quite simply unable to spend an evening alone, and would cease to love anyone who was unable to be with her constantly and whom she could not trust would never abandon her. . . . All in all, I love her very, very much—far more than she loves me—but I cannot take on the role of ever-present male nursemaid (although she absolutely would have loved me for it); for this price I could be her husband, but I am afraid I would be unable to sustain such a role, and what would the poor creature do then?

Sofia, for her part, complained that her husband was always immersed in his books: "He needs only a book and a cup of tea in order to feel completely satisfied."

SOFIA KOVALEVSKAYA. WERE you jealous of the books that stole Vladimir's attention? Did you feel demoted to the bottom of the list of his passions?

Perhaps you began to disturb him at work, imposing unreasonable demands on him in order to make him prioritize you?

Did you insist that he accompany you to conferences because you did not dare travel alone? Did not trust yourself? Were afraid of getting lost?

Did he have to help you with practical errands you found insufferable, like buying formal outfits for special occasions? And selecting shoes?

Maybe you even demanded to know the first letters of the names of everyone he'd ever been in love with?

THE RELATIONSHIP BETWEEN Sofia and Vladimir was not entirely platonic, for the couple had a daughter in 1878, ten years after they had married. Despite the fact that a few years earlier Vladimir had indicated that one of the reasons for the couple's lack of physical intimacy was the fear of children:

> In my opinion, Sofia absolutely cannot become a mother. It would quite simply destroy her, and she too fears this herself; it would tear her away from her work and make her miserable.

When the couple's daughter was four years old, Vladimir took his own life after getting mixed up with a gang of Russian swindlers who ruined him. Even though they no longer lived together, Sofia mourned so intensely that she locked herself away in her room. She upbraided herself. Refused to eat. After five days, she lost consciousness. A doctor had to force-feed her.

When she was finally able to sit upright in bed again, she asked for a pen and paper. "I need only touch mathematics, and then I forget everything else on earth," she said. It was during this period that she began the work that won her the prestigious Bordin Prize from the Academy of Sciences in Paris in 1888. Her work was of such a high standard that the committee decided to increase the prize money from 3,000 to 5,000 francs.

When her sister, Anyuta, died a few years after Vladimir, Sofia sought refuge in her work once again. But this time, mathematics could not save her. This time, she wrote literature—her novel about the two Raevsky sisters.

In a letter to Gösta Mittag-Leffler, Sofia expressed the weighty thoughts she was struggling with:

> How abominable life is, and how ridiculous it is to continue to live. . . . So much is said about the perfection of the organism—the way in which, little by little, living creatures have developed through natural selection and the survival of the fittest. I rather think that the most desirable perfection would be the ability to die a quick and easy death.

YOU WERE JUST as unhappy as me. Even though you were married. Even though you had a daughter.

Just imagine if Jakob had chosen differently and ended up as unhappy as Vladimir—ended up taking his own life—because he couldn't live with having abandoned his children. It's better that he still exists here in the world. Even if I can never see him again.

Perhaps Jakob was right. Maybe you didn't have a romantic relationship with Weierstrass after all.

I seem to interpret everything as love.

THEN HILDE COMES into Rakel's life. At the end of January, Hilde comes to the Blue City to read from the novel she's just published. It's one of the universe's magical moments, when you suddenly see yourself in another. See one of the other versions of yourself—who you might have been, had the building blocks only been stacked in a different order.

Hilde talks about her life. How she started to study mathematics, but fell ill. That's why she started to write. She moved back home to her parents', where she lay in a dark room for several years, fearing that her life was over, that this was how the rest of her life would be. The two letters of the diagnosis made her feel that she was participating in a reversed EM. The European Masters for couch potatoes. Only for eternal optimists and the most persevering. Those who have to live with the distrust of the medical community and the suspicions of their peers. As if they aren't trying to do their best. When the real problem is that they have been doing their best for much too long. Till their body breaks down.

Hilde and Rakel. Their lives are like mirror images of each other. From literature to mathematics, from mathematics to literature. The extremes in them. Loving too hard, falling too deep. Dreaming so big that they're continuously disappointed. It isn't the voice and language she recognizes in Hilde. This time, it's the universe itself. Something about black holes, gravity making time pass more slowly, layers upon layers on top of each other, the literary quotations, the letters she writes in English, the need to embrace herself.

Hilde, who read *In Search of Lost Time* in order to find out how Proust makes time pass more slowly. Hilde, the second person she's ever met to embody epsilon. Hilde, who gives her a copy of her novel with the finest dedication Rakel can imagine:

To Rakel—we're connected, you and me.

To recognize oneself. To resemble another. To be connected.

Hilde gives her faith that it might help to write about the things she's most ashamed of, the things she doesn't tell anyone. It will be a novel she wouldn't want anyone to read, and one it will only be possible to publish after her death. But that's precisely why it feels so freeing to write it.

Maybe writing is about finding your way to life's essential moments and holding on to them? And then pulling the right threads that can connect them all together. Like a spider's web. It's actually quite simple. She just needs to weave one thread at a time. The colors first, then the characters.

Hilde leads a discussion with two female authors at Bjørnsonhuset. She asks one of them: "Where were you when you began to write this book, and where did you want to go?"

This is how Rakel discovers it. To write is to want to change yourself, to want to change something in your life. To wish to be somewhere other than where you are at that particular moment. Maybe that's why you can't be too content if you are to feel the urge to write?

You are going to feel the need to write, but let it come when it must. Do something else first.

BLACK HOLES IN space, the imprints of dead stars. Where gravity is so strong that it becomes impossible to escape once you've been caught. Then you'll be pulled into the black hole in a spiraling motion. Because gravity is so strong that even time itself is stretched out and passes more slowly in the vicinity of black holes.

But maybe the holes aren't completely black after all. Rakel finds an article about Hawking radiation. The theory, published by Stephen Hawking the year she was born, which posits that some particles are in fact able to escape black holes. That heat can radiate from black holes. And that the temperature in the hole actually increases when it radiates heat. So that in the end, the black hole will explode in an eruption of gamma rays and disappear completely.

RAKEL LIES IN bed, imagining the final scene of the movie about Sofia Kovalevskaya and Weierstrass. The film she once had plans of shooting with Jakob.

The camera focuses on the nameplate on Weierstrass's door in Berlin. Potsdammer Strasse 40. A woman's hand knocks at the door. The housekeeper opens it. Her face is twenty years older than when Sofia first knocked on the door. This time, she smiles and lets Sofia in straightaway. The camera follows Sofia's shoes down the dim corridor. But they don't stop outside the door to Weierstrass's study. Instead, they continue up a staircase and stop at the door to his bedroom.

"He's extremely ill," the housekeeper whispers. "But he's looking forward to seeing you."

Weierstrass lifts his head from the pillow as Sofia enters the room. The camera zooms in on his face. He's pale, but it's clear that he's happy to see her. Sofia kneels beside the bed and buries her face in the covers. Her shoulders shake. Is she crying because she hasn't visited him earlier, that she has let so many years go by? That she hasn't responded to the letters he sent her?

Weierstrass lays a hand on her head. She turns her face, so she can look him in the eye.

"Why did it never come to anything between us?" she asks.

"There was always something between us," he says.

"But why didn't you come to Bolanzo?"

"I hoped you would find a younger man than me," he says. "Someone who could make you happier."

He starts to cough. She rises, and takes the cloth from where it hangs over the headboard. Bends over him, and wipes the beads of sweat from his brow.

"Do you think we'll meet in the next life?" she asks.

"I don't believe in the reincarnation of souls," he says.

"But if you're wrong?" she says. "If we're reborn as new copies of ourselves?"

"Then I promise to look for you."

"What if you don't recognize me?"

"Of course I'll recognize you," he says. "The girl with the golden eyes, that gild everything and everyone you look at."

She sighs. "Our story would have made a fine romance novel, don't you think?"

He allows his gaze to rest on her for a long time. Those wise St. Bernard eyes. "We're probably more suited to a novel about loneliness, you and I," he says finally.

The camera fades out. As if the light has been extinguished, as if the film ends here. But then it isn't the end after all. A faint crackling can be heard, along with the sound of someone crying. The camera follows the sound, and we see Weierstrass, sitting before the tiled stove in only his nightgown, a pile of letters in his hands.

He's just received word that Sofia is dead, that she died a few days after arriving home in Stockholm. He's now burning the letters she sent to him, one by one. But not before he has read them one last time. The camera zooms in on the flame in the tiled stove, as if following his gaze. In the flame, brief glimpses from Sofia's life flicker past, fragments of the film we have already seen.

Before the credits roll, we learn that Weierstrass lived for another six years, confined to a wheelchair. And that he never got over the loss of Sofia.

SOFIA WAS CELEBRATED for her achievements in mathematics, receiving prizes and recognition not granted to many other women. She was admired by the greatest mathematicians of the age, such as Weierstrass and Poincaré, but also by contemporary authors, such as Ibsen, Dostoevsky, Turgenev, and Tolstoy.

She captivated Fridtjof Nansen so intensely at their first meeting that Nansen later confided to a friend that if things had been different and he hadn't already been engaged to someone else, Sofia might have played a decisive role in his life. Nansen had already become interested in Sofia through a description of her in a letter from a friend: "She laughs like a child, smiles like a wise woman, masters the art of speaking aloud only some of her thoughts and letting silence communicate the rest. I have never met her equal."

Dostoevsky likely based the character of Alexandra in *The Idiot* on Sofia. Turgenev used her as the physical inspiration for Marianna in *Virgin Soil*. George Eliot described her as "a pretty creature with charming modest voice and speech, who is studying Mathematics." Ibsen described her using the following words: "Her life can only be depicted poetically."

But according to Sofia, the Norwegian novelist Jonas Lie was the only person to ever truly understand her. He didn't refer to her as a great mathematician, and he didn't even describe her as a successful author. He spoke of her as the little girl he had become extremely fond of and for whom he felt such intense sympathy after having read her childhood memoirs. He felt so sorry for this little neglected child, who longed so intensely for affection and who was never understood by anyone. Life had showered her with gifts that held no value for her: honor, distinctions, success. But it had refused her the things she wanted most of all. So she remained as she had been as a child, with her big, wide-open eyes, longing for a touch of affection. Standing there, her hands outstretched and empty.

Although all the great men idolized her, none of them truly wanted her. They didn't need her in the way she needed to be needed. "He loved me only when he was with me, but he could so easily have managed to live apart from me," she once said of a man. Sofia's downfall was perhaps that she expected too much of those who loved her, that she was too intense. That she wanted to be their whole world.

Toward the end of her life, Sofia entered into a stormy relationship with the sociologist Maxim Kovalevsky. He came to Stockholm to give a series of lectures after having been stripped of his professorship in Moscow. According to Sofia, Maxim was the perfect fictional hero. "Never before have I been so tempted to write a romance novel as when in Maxim's presence," she wrote. "He is so great, so 'gross geschlagen,' that he takes up a terrible amount of space, both on the divan and in one's mind. It is simply impossible for me to think about anything else when he is near."

It must have been easy for Sofia to convince herself that a man who carried her own surname must have been meant for her, that this was a sign that fate had finally granted her the man who would be hers. Maxim proposed, but demanded that she give up her work. Sofia couldn't do this, but neither could she release herself from him. She was trapped in an impossible situation, a circle from which she could never break free.

They argued at his villa in Genoa, and she spent a cold day out in the rain and the wind. On her way back to Stockholm, she contracted pneumonia and died just a few days after arriving home.

Upon receiving word of her death, Anne Charlotte Leffler thought that Sofia must have taken her own life. Sofia believed in the immortality and rebirth of the soul, and had told Anne Charlotte that it was only fear of punishment in the next life that prevented her from leaving this world voluntarily.

The last thing Sofia said to her mathematician friend Leo Königsberger, when visiting him on her way home to Stockholm just days before she died, was this: "A woman is only happy when men prostrate themselves at her feet. Perhaps I would have been happier had I been an authoress!"

To stake one's heart on love is also a form of suicide, thinks Rakel.

SHE CAN'T TELL Jakob what she has found out about Sofia Kovalevskaya. He may never finish his novel. But she understands that Sofia had a black hole within her, and that in the end, this hole could no longer be filled with mathematics alone. It had to be filled with literature too. And with love fit to make one's heart burst.

This incessant hope for love, life-giving and murderous at the same time. Which makes people walk in eternal circles, with this hope as the luminous center. If only it were a downward spiral instead. At least then there would be a chance to discover that it's all about turning and moving in the opposite direction in order to get out of the labyrinth, away from the black hole. People who get lost in the desert end up walking in circles when they think they are walking straight ahead. Perdition is an inextricable part of human nature. You need something to give you a nudge in the right direction, so you cross over onto the tangent that leads out of the circle. Otherwise, you'll continue to circle hope for all eternity, like a lost satellite in orbit around a dying star.

WHAT IF TIME is not a straight number line, but a coiled-up spiral? Where the centuries lie against one another, separated only by thin membranes. If you set your ear against the membrane, you might hear vibrations from the other side, from those who were here before, and those who will come after. Would Sofia have felt less lonely, had she thought this way? If she had known that Rakel is lying on the other side of the membrane, listening to the sound of her breathing?

Sofia, who lies in bed with pneumonia and knows that her life is over. Maybe she dreams of being reborn as Rakel? Invents scenes from Rakel's life, instead of thinking of her own death? What ending would Sofia have imagined for Rakel's story? Something open? Something that could be both light and dark at the same time?

THE SPACE BETWEEN F sharp and G flat. The space to which she must find the key in order to be able to write. Perhaps the space between F sharp and G flat is inside her? A tiny change in perspective? A shift from minor to major?

Meeting Hilde has opened something in her; it feels as if something has worked loose in there. As if a stage curtain has been raised. She can clearly see how everything has a fractal structure. The writing process, where the same themes appear over and over again, until you finally recognize the patterns and reach an understanding. Love, where you rediscover the same qualities in the people you become fond of, only with a slight twist. And life, strange and surprising life, that simply keeps going, on and on, in new people with the same longings, timeless for all time.

Maybe she can use mathematics in her writing? Perhaps she can give her novel a fractal structure? A collection of expanded moments. Fragmented and full of holes, where parts of the story repeat, only with a slight twist, as if from another perspective. Several copies reflecting each other—in different time frames and with varying levels of detail. Magnifications and reductions. Layer upon layer, one on top of the other. Alternately golden and gray.

Almost like a Cantor set: take the story, divide it into three, and remove the middle portion. We're then left with two parts; gold first, granite last. Then we repeat the process on each of the parts: more gold and more granite. In the end, the pieces of gold and granite become so small that it's impossible to tell them apart. Then the story will have a golden sheen. Because even though there's mostly granite, the gold shines more brightly.

If only she could be given all the strength she has left in this life at once, have it all apportioned to her at the same time. If only she could have one month when she feels almost well. Then she'll never ask for anything else. Then she will be ready.

SHE STARTS WRITING at the beginning of March, the month of light and progress. When the days increase most quickly in length, and when time is turned one hour ahead. It's as if the words have lain within her, maturing, for years, and when she strikes the first chord, and finds the keynote, they pour out of her. She can't write quickly enough and wakes several times during the night to note down keywords, so she won't forget what she has thought; feels that she just has to go with the flow, writing down the words uncritically as they come, now while she's in flux. She can always go back and change things later.

This is the meaning of her life. This was what she was meant to do. She knows it now, with absolute certainty.

You are going to feel the need to write, but let it come when it must. Do something else first.

"Everything I have written about I've had to experience—both in my body and with my soul," said the novelist Mikkjel Fønhus.

All this I have suffered in order to show you love, thinks Rakel.

She marks the final period nineteen years to the day that she received Jakob's first letter, where he wrote that she has excellent taste in problems. The day after she spoke to him in the cafeteria for the very first time. And nineteen, after all, is her lucky number.

IN THE AFTERNOON, she takes a walk to Kringstadsetra with Pappa. It's Good Friday. When they have walked all the way back down to the fields at Kringstad farm, the fields where she once wrote a letter to the sky and received a reply, she catches sight of something moving out on the fjord. The water is dead calm. But there's something moving out there all the same.

"What's that?" she asks.

Pappa doesn't know.

She walks closer. "It's just three ducks," she says. "And here's me, hoping that it might be a porpoise."

"I thought you meant the pattern on the water," says Pappa.

And then she sees it, the cross on the water's surface. The interference pattern formed by the waves because of their slight differences in direction and length. A large and clear cross, with the ducks as three small dots at the center.

"It's a cross," she exclaims. "On Good Friday itself."

It must be a sign. There's no reasonable explanation for why the currents of the fjord should form such a pattern right there. Even Pappa is struck by it.

A cross on Good Friday. As if to remind her that suffering too can make time pass more slowly. Make life seem longer. Make a Friday unbearably long. *All this I have suffered in order to show you love.* Perhaps Jesus also had this thought as he hung there on the cross.

FERRIES CROSSING ON the fjord. Coming toward one another, each from its own side, meeting and becoming one before they slowly slide away from each other again. Pappa called them "crossing ferries" and timed how long it took from when the ferries met until they parted ways.

"Nineteen point eight seconds," he said, satisfied. Rakel called them "kissing ferries" and hoped that they would last for a long, long time.

She takes the time. Nineteen years and eight hours, she thinks. It will do.

IN ORDER TO walk away from someone you love, every organ in the body must be notified. It is not enough for the brain to have made up its mind. Because the heart can make the body turn around. Just as the lips, the uterus, the diaphragm, the nape of the neck, the lobes of the ears, the eyelids, the backs of the knees, the toes, the iliac crest— yes, even the navel—can make the body turn around. As can those treacherous spaces in between, where imprints of the loved one might be concealed. The gap between nameless toes. The distance between the chin and the base of the throat. The space between the labia.

Come, my friends. Come with me now. I need each and every one of you. And you must never look back.

Two lungs, leaving. Four chambers of the heart, twelve pairs of ribs, thirty-four vertebrae, and a tailbone. Two dimples on the lower back, ten tender fingertips. Twenty-six feet of intestine, four quarts of blood, and twenty-two square feet of skin. All leaving, moving away.

Knowing this: *Without him, I have no one. Without him, I am no one. Because without him, I do not know who I am.* And still forcing oneself farther away. The spinal cord, the cerebellum—yes, the entire central nervous system—must obey this singular command: We will move on. And never look back.

A NOTE ON THE STRUCTURE
OF THE NOVEL

When I started writing this novel, I was at a dark place in life. Health problems had forced me to give up my position as a research mathematician at the University of Oslo, and I had to spend a lot of time in bed. I wanted to find something I could do even though I had very little energy. As I have always enjoyed writing, I decided to write a few sentences every day, to give myself something to look forward to. I ended up with lots of small text fragments, but they didn't seem to fit together as a whole.

Then I got the idea that I could try to use mathematics as a literary device, not only in the contents of the story, but also in the composition. During my PhD, I had worked on geometric objects called fractals. Fractals are built up of smaller copies of themselves, and it struck me that they are also quite fragmented, but the fragments are connected through reflections and repetitions. This gave me the idea that I could try to link my text fragments in a similar way; that I could build a mosaic by using repetitions, parallels, and reflections. I decided to have two female mathematicians in my novel, Rakel Havberg in our time and Sofia Kovalevskaya in the nineteenth century, and let their lives interweave and reflect each other the same way the smaller copies of a fractal resemble the same general shape, but may have variations.

Once I got this idea, the fractal structure seemed to evolve naturally. The same elements started to appear several places, both early and late in the text, both in Sofia's and Rakel's life, but often with new interpretations. Sometimes it's the images that are the same, other times it may be sentences and even whole paragraphs that are repeated with small variations. In some sense it feels like the fractal structure emerged from the patterns of life, with everything that is repeated and propagated through history and generations.

But I could just as well describe the structure of this novel as being sparked by classical music. I was particularly inspired by the violin sonata in A major by César Frank, in how the same theme keeps reoccurring with small variations—it is transformed, modulated, and inverted. But also, in how effortlessly the piece changes between major and minor keys. I wanted my novel to have some of the same qualities; having both light and darkness present at the same time, so closely interwoven that it would be hard to tell if it is actually a story of love or a story of loneliness.

Some readers may have noticed that the name of the protagonist, Rakel Havberg, is a permutation of the letters in my own name. I think of Rakel as my dark twin. She has the same starting point in life as myself and many of the same building blocks, but they are put together in a different order. I took pieces from my own life and started playing with them. Gradually Rakel took on a life of her own and started doing things that surprised me. Her personality was influenced by Sofia Kovalevskaya, who was very strong and at the same time extremely vulnerable. Sofia was also quite superstitious, and suddenly Rakel started to see patterns and connections that might not actually exist.

When I finished writing the novel and had to let go of Rakel's company, I missed her. Sometimes there is a lot of comfort in a protagonist whose problems are worse than your own. But I am happy that she will now be able to travel out into the world and meet new people. Perhaps she'll find someone she can comfort and keep company.

AUTHOR'S NOTE

In working on this book I have been inspired by the life of Sofia Kovalevskaya (1850–91), and much of the material about her is taken from her childhood memoirs (*Ur ryska lifvet: Systrarna Rajevski*, Hæggström, 1889) and from the biography Anne Charlotte Leffler published about her in the year after she died (*Sonja Kovalevsky: Hvad jag upplefvat tillsammans med henne och vad hon berättat mig om sig själf*, Albert Bonniers Förlag, 1892).

I have quoted excerpts from the letters exchanged between Sofia Kovalevskaya and Karl Weierstrass, which can be found in the archives of the Mittag-Leffler Institute in Djursholm, Sweden, and which have been published in German (Reinhard Bölling, ed., *Briefwechsel zwischen Karl Weierstrass und Sofja Kowalewskaja*, Wiley-VCH, 1993). Sofia's other letters (including those exchanged with Gösta Mittag-Leffler) are also held by the Mittag-Leffler Institute.

I have also made use of excerpts of the letters exchanged between Vladimir Kovalevsky and his brother Alexander (S. Shtraikh, *Sestry Korvin-Krukovskie*, Moscow, 1933), the memoirs of Josef Malevich (*Sofia Vasilevna Kovalevskaia, doktor filosofii i professor vysshei matematiki*, "Vospominiiakh pervogo, po vremeni, ee uchitelia I.I. Malevicha, 1858–1869," *Russkaia Starina*, no. 12 [1890]: 615–54), and the memoirs of Julia Lermontova (quoted in Anne Charlotte Leffler's biography about Sofia from 1892, and recounted in Russian in S. Shtraikh, *Vospominanija o Sof'e Kovalevskoj*, 1951, 375–87). The originals can be found in the Russian State Archive of Literature and Art (Rossiiskii Gosudarstvennyi Arkhiv Literatury i Iskusstva [RGALI], Moscow). Parts of these texts have been translated into English (including in Don H. Kennedy, *Little Sparrow: A Portrait of Sophia Kovalevsky*, Ohio University Press, 1983, and in Ann H. Koblitz, *Sofia Kovalevskaia: Scientist, Writer, Revolutionary*, Birkhäuser, 1983).

I have also used brief quotations from the memoirs of Sophie Adelung ("Jugenderinnerungen an Sophie Kowalewsky," *Deutsche Rundschau* 89 [1896]: 394–425; http://archiv.ub.uni-heidelberg.de/volltextserver/13162/1/Kowalewsky_adelung.pdf), Leo Königsberger (*Mein Leben*, Carl Winters Universitätsbuchhandlung, 1919, 117; http://histmath-heidelberg.de/txt/koenigsberger/leben.htm), and Marie Mendelson ("Briefe von Sophie Kowalewska," *Neue Deutsche Rundschau*, no. 6 [1897]: 589–614).

This is, however, first and foremost a novel, with all the freedoms this affords. The adaptation and translations of the various quotations into Norwegian have therefore been undertaken by the author in collaboration with the novel's protagonist, Rakel, in order to view the material through her eyes.

This book would never have been completed without the people who have helped and supported me throughout the process of writing it. The greatest thanks are due to my wise, enthusiastic, and caring editors Hilde Rød-Larsen and Nora Campbell. To Hilde, who renewed my belief in this project when I needed it most, made countless suggestions for improvements along the way, and loved the very best sides of the book's protagonist, Rakel, into being. And to Nora, who continually inspired me to stretch myself further, who helped me to find out what my novel was actually about, and who made invaluable contributions in the book's final phase. Thanks also to the rest of the enthusiastic team at my publishers, Aschehoug.

A special thank you to Arild Stubhaug, who helped me find the original text of one of the letters in the Mittag-Leffler Institute's archives.

Warm thanks to all the people who in various ways have encouraged, supported, comforted, and nudged me throughout the writing process: Dag, Eirin, Emmy, Eva, Georgina, Heidi, Henning, Jan, Jostein,

Kjersti, Magnhild, Rasmus, Tom, Vania, Viktor, and Vivi. And last, but not least: thanks to Mamma and Pappa, who have always been there for me. This book is dedicated to you.

Klara Hveberg
Molde, September 2018

A NOTE FROM THE TRANSLATOR

Translation is always a balancing act, but I found this to be especially true while working on Klara Hveberg's beautiful, multi-layered novel of loss, longing, and mathematics, which presented a number of challenges. The greatest of these was posed by the novel's structure—readers are taken on a fractal, spiraling journey as again and again Rakel revisits her understanding of herself and her place in the world, gaining new insights into and perspectives on her illness, her loneliness, the passage of time and what it means to love. Her thoughts and the events of her life mirror and are reflected in the life of Sofia Kovalevskaya, creating echoes and thematic associations for the reader that are a huge part of what makes the book so fascinating. This effect is partly achieved through the precise repetition of certain phrases in various scenes and contexts, which necessitated finding English phrases that would work equally in all these contexts in the same way as in the Norwegian, while remaining as close to the original as possible. Another technique employed by the author in the creation of this effect is a fluid switching between past and present tense in the narration of the various sections—something that can feel much more jarring in English than it does in Norwegian. But the rendering of Rakel's memories and past events in the present tense gives the novel a freshness and immediacy that it felt vital not to lose in the translation, and so a balance had to be found here, too.

On top of this came the challenges presented by Rakel's unique voice and the novel's mathematical subject matter. Rakel's thought processes are central to the book: she has a thought. Which leads her onto another thought, and then another. Recreating the experience of being inside Rakel's head in English, without the text sounding too stilted, was again a balancing act. There is a certain naivety to Rakel, but at the same time she explores highly complex mathematical concepts and relates them in an understandable way. An extremely rewarding working relationship with the author assisted me in finding the correct terminology and best ways to present these concepts, and we had great fun experimenting with the novel's instances of wordplay. One of the things I admire most about the novel is the line it treads between the simple and the complex, the everyday and the profound, and the way this is expressed through the poetic simplicity and rhythm of the Norwegian. One of my aims in translating any text is to give readers a reading experience that mirrors my own in reading the original, and that felt especially important here when recreating the author's style.

One final and perhaps surprising challenge I found myself grappling with is that which comes with translating a text for which you feel a special personal affinity and affection—that extra sense of responsibility and the desire to do the text justice in another language, to get it right. This is the only time in my career to date that I have been moved to tears while working on a book—I was so touched by Rakel's curiosity, vulnerability and determination, and the beauty of the language in which her story is told. I hope readers will enjoy visiting (and revisiting) Rakel's inner world as much as I enjoyed working on the translation—this is a novel that bears rereading, offering new revelations each time.

Alison McCullough

REFERENCES TO NORWEGIAN LITERATURE

The lyrics on pages 9 and 10 are taken from "Nøtteliten," a song by Alf Prøysen (slightly rewritten to fit Rakel's misconceptions).

The lyrics on page 15 are taken from "Easter Morning Quenches Sorrow" ("Påskemorgen slukker sorgen"), a psalm by N. F. S. Grundtvig.

The lyrics on page 17, "Took a little nugget of gold, with a hop-hop-skip, with a hop-hop-skip" ("Tok en liten gullklump, skipskipskara, skipskipskara, skipskipskara"), are taken from the song "Flew a Little Bluebird" ("Fløy en liten blåfugl"), a Norwegian trad.

The lines on page 32, "the fox that hurried over the rice," are in reference to "The Fox Hurries over the Ice" ("Reven rasker over isen"), a Norwegian trad.

The lines on pages 33 and 184 are in reference to *A Doll's House* (*Et dukkehjem*), a play by Henrik Ibsen.

The line on page 71, "You I would in rhythms fondly rivet tight" ("Deg vil jeg ømt i rytmer nagle fast"), is the opening line of "Metope," a poem by Olaf Bull.

The line on page 72, "From now on I'll walk you all the way home" ("Heretter følger jeg deg helt hjem"), is the title of a short story by Kjell Askildsen.

The lines on pages 77 and 78 are taken from "Summer Passed Quickly This Year" ("Sommeren gikk fort i år"), a poem by Stein Mehren (slightly rewritten).

The lyrics on page 133 are taken from "Lullaby for a Little Boy" ("Vuggevise for lillegutt"), a song by Per Winge under the pen name Garberg (slightly rewritten).

The lines on page 138 are taken from "A Great Love Never Dies" ("En stor kjærlighet dør aldri") and from "Meeting" ("Møte"), both poems by Stein Mehren.

The line on page 142, "Lean your loneliness quietly against mine" ("Lene din ensomhet stille mot min"), is taken from a poem by Stein Mehren (slightly rewritten).

The lines on page 147, "Love is the origin of the world and its ruler, but all its ways are filled with flowers and blood, flowers and blood." ("Og kjærligheten ble verdens opphav og verdens hersker; men alle dens veier er fulle av blomster og blod, blomster og blod"), are taken from *Victoria*, a novel by Knut Hamsun.

The line on page 208, "Frihedens tale til Moldenserne" ("Liberty's Speech to the Citizens of Molde"), is in reference to an article by Bjørnstjerne Bjørnson, *Romsdals Budstikke*, May 12, 1848.

The lines on page 222, *"Of moonlight nothing grows"* (*"Av måneskinn gror det ingenting"*), is the title of a novel by Torborg Nedreaas.

The lines on page 263, "But the human heart remains the same all through the ages" ("Men menneskenes hjerter forandres aldeles intet i alle dager"), are taken from *Tales of King Arthur and the Knights of the Round Table* (*Fortellinger om Kong Artur og Ridderne av Det runde bord*), a collection of short stories by Sigrid Undset.

Here ends Klara Hveberg's
Lean Your Loneliness Slowly Against Mine.

The first edition of this book was printed and bound at
Grafica Veneta in Trebaseleghe, Italy, August 2021.

A NOTE ON THE TYPE

The text of this novel was set in Dante, a typeface first
developed by German-Italian printer and type designer
Giovanni Mardersteig (1892–1977), founder of private press
Officina Bodoni. Officina Bodoni quickly gained a repu-
tation for their high-quality printing, and Mardesteig approached typefaces with the same perfectionism. Dante
was released for mechanical composition in 1957. The dig-
ital version, which you see on this page, was redrawn by
Monotype's Ron Carpenter and released in 1993. Dante is
an exquisite, balanced serif font, making it perfect for print.

HarperVia

An imprint dedicated to publishing international voices,
offering readers a chance to encounter other lives and other
points of view via the language of the imagination.